# The Mystery
# at Black Horse Farm

Jenny Hughes

# The Mystery
# at Black Horse Farm

Published by Pony, Stabenfeldt A/S
Cover  and inside illustration: Jennifer Bell
Cover layout: Stabenfeldt AS
Edited by Bobbie Chase
Printed in Norway
ISBN: 82-591-1168-3

# Chapter One

I'd seen Oliver before the summer camp at **Black Horse Farm,** of course. He lived in a different part of town, but we'd sometimes competed at the same horse shows, not against each other exactly – he'd be in the prestigious Open Jumping while Flint and I were in one of the smaller ring's Novice Classes. Oliver had often smiled in my direction as he rode out after yet another clear round. It was the kind of smile that buckled my knees and turned my insides to jelly, but I'd never gotten close enough to see if I had the same effect on him. I needed to get to know him better and could hardly believe my luck when my dad remarked casually that not only was Oliver going to the same summer pony camp as I, but also we were to travel there and back together!

"How – how did that happen, then?" I tried to look cool as I threw some more T-shirts into my bag.

"His father and I got talking." He eyed my mounting color curiously. "You've gone very red, Yasmine, are you OK?"

"Just a bit hot." I bent my head forward so my long hair would cover my face. "I didn't realize you two knew each other."

"I see him at the gym. Nice guy. As soon as I said you and Flint were going to **Black Horse Farm** he said we could share the transportation. He's going to take you there, and I'll collect you both."

I was so excited I was nearly sick.

"Good idea," I said coolly. "It saves us having to hire a trailer, doesn't it?"

"Yup. Oliver goes to so many shows they need to have their own. They'll pick you up in the morning, if you're sure you don't mind going with them."

"I don't mind." I couldn't wait for him to go so I could dance around my bedroom, punching the air and saying, '*YES! YES!*' under my breath.

You'd think with the kind of build up I'd given it that the actual getting-to-know-Oliver bit would be a total anticlimax or even a disaster, but it wasn't. From the minute he arrived, hopping out of his dad's car to help me load Flint he was – well, just **gorgeous.**

Flint, my beautiful black pony, was as good as gold walking into the trailer, and Oliver said a lot of complimentary things about him, which made me like him (Oliver, I mean) even more. The journey down to the West coast where the summer camp was situated took about two hours, and I think we talked the whole way. Oliver was very funny, telling me about the falls and disasters he'd suffered in his riding career so far. He was very modest about his undoubted skill, never mentioning the many cups and rosettes I knew he'd won.

"They have a show jumping competition at the camp." I was so looking forward to the vacation I knew the schedule by heart. "But I won't stand a chance if everyone else is as good as you and Lincoln," I said.

"Lincoln's brilliant," he agreed. "I'm lucky to have a horse who loves jumping so much. But don't put yourself down, Yasmine. I've watched you and Flint, and you've both got a lot of talent."

"Oh, well." I did the old hiding behind the hair trick again. "I'm sure it'll be fun, no matter how badly we do."

We were getting on so well that the time passed in a flash and I could hardly believe it when Oliver's father said "Here's the sign for **Black Horse Farm**. Not long now."

It was a beautiful place, tucked away in a quiet valley below the sheltering downs, its honey colored stone blending into the soft golds and greens of the surrounding countryside. The first thing to do, obviously, was get Flint and Lincoln settled. There was a lovely old stable yard, very neat and professional looking, and we checked our horses over thoroughly before leaving them to rest with nice deep beds of straw and a hay net each.

"You can turn them out in one of the paddocks later, if you'd prefer," June Preston, the co-owner of the farm said, smiling at us both.

She was nice, plump and motherly, with a mass of unruly blonde hair and that unmistakable 'proper horsy person' air about her. Oliver and I were taken over to the farmhouse and shown our rooms. Then we made our way to the big, sunlit kitchen downstairs at the back of the house. Some of the other summer campers were already there: we met sisters Jessica and Mandy, who seemed friendly, plus a cheerful Lee aged about fourteen like us, his pal Chas, and Grant, a dark and moody-looking fifteen-year-old who was even taller than Oliver.

"There are a few more kids arriving later – we have a dozen booked." June was helping at the stove where a small, mousy haired lady, introduced as Maureen, was stirring something that smelled wonderful. "But in the meantime I expect you're all starving, so lunch won't be long."

It was really pleasant sitting in the sunny kitchen, drinking Maureen's delicious homemade soup, munching on warm crusty bread and listening to everyone talking and laughing. I tend to listen quite a lot; I suppose I'm a bit shy 'til I get to know people properly. Oliver was brilliant; joining in with everyone but talking to me the most, which made me feel all girly and glowing. The sullen-looking Grant didn't have much to say, but when June looked out of the window and announced, "Oh good, Hayley's back," I saw him sit up expectantly.

"Hayley's our daughter," June told us. "She's been helping her dad put the finishing touches on our cross country course. You're our first visitors, and we want everything to be perfect for you."

I was thinking happily that perfect was just how I'd describe it when the door burst open and Hayley came bouncing in. I don't mean she was fat or anything, in fact she was slim and tiny, but she moved with so much energy she made you think of an exuberant rubber ball. She had the same tousled blonde curls as her mother, a pretty, heart shaped face and incredibly blue eyes.

"Ooh, great!" she beamed happily at Oliver and me. "More visitors! Hi, I'm Hayley. You must be Oliver and Yasmine. You're a great looking couple. Is Oliver your boyfriend, Yasmine?"

9

"No," I said shortly, going red with embarrassment.

"Ignore her, hon." June plunked a bowl of soup rather crossly in front of her daughter. "Hayley always dives in with both feet first."

"Sorry." The girl seemed quite unrepentant. "I was only saying they look good together. How's everyone else doing?"

They all started chattering again. I could see they all liked Hayley, and to my secret dismay even Oliver leaned back in his chair smiling as he listened to her description of the course-building she'd been doing. She was a natural flirt, but it seemed to me that more was directed to Oliver than anyone else. The heavily-built Grant seemed to notice this too, and made several attempts at distracting her away from talking to Oliver. My heart sank at the thought of competing for Oliver's attention with such a pretty, bubbly blonde, and I felt my confidence ebbing away. He was bound to prefer her, I told myself, so I should stop thinking we were on the point of establishing a really good relationship.

I started to feel less shy when we all went out for a ride around the farm's grounds later that day. At first it was fabulous. Oliver rode his rangy bay, Lincoln, alongside me while June pointed out any interesting landmarks. Opening a big, heavy gate, she led us through to a shady lane leading, she told us, to the beautiful downs that surrounded **Black Horse Farm**.

"We only just moved here ourselves," she explained, "and I haven't had time to explore many routes, but I'm sure you'll find riding out from here is just great."

She was right. The downs were glorious, and as Flint and Lincoln cantered side-by-side across the springy turf, I felt my high spirits returning and vowed to push away the stab of jealousy I'd felt over Hayley. Oliver looked as though he was enjoying himself too, grinning at me as my black pony tried with all his might to overtake the bigger bay.

"Lincoln's part Thoroughbred, I'll have you know," he yelled in mock severity. "So how come it's your pony who thinks he's a race horse?"

It was true, Flint was straining every muscle as we thundered along, and I joined in with Oliver's laughter, reveling in the sense of speed and power as Flint forged ahead. It was a fabulous ride, and when we turned and started back at a sensible, cooling down walk, I was feeling just great again. Oliver had hardly left my side, turning occasionally to talk to some of the others, but mainly seeming quite content to be with me. Hayley, riding mostly with Grant and the other boys, was very confident in the way she handled her big chestnut mare, Sika, getting her to execute perfect turns on the forehand as she rode back and forth, doing as her mother told her and checking that

11

everyone was OK. She talked non-stop the whole time, giving everyone her beaming, cheerful smile and encouraging the more timid Jessica and Mandy to relax and enjoy themselves. I decided I'd been paranoid, being scared she would make Oliver her main target and that, if she did, he'd dump me immediately. Even so, when we were back on **Black Horse Farm** land and she rode towards us looking conspiratorial, my heart sank.

"We're going to have a sneak preview of the cross country course, and take the jumping route through the next bit of woods. Want to come along?"

My heart sank even further. We'd looked at a couple of the fences, and to my inexperienced eye they looked frighteningly big and solid. I was sure Oliver would want to, though, so I said hastily, "You go Oliver, I'll – um – wait 'til June takes us around. "

He hesitated briefly. "No, I'll stay with you, Yasmine."

Hayley pulled a comic face of disapproval. "Grant said you'd chicken out."

"Oh, this is Grant's plan, is it?" Oliver said, looking a bit grim. "Well, I don't think it's a good idea without your Mom knowing."

For a moment I thought Hayley wavered, but when Grant called her she spun Sika defiantly and followed him at a smart canter into a copse over to our right.

Oliver shook his head and brought Lincoln, who'd started to dance excitedly, back to a walk.

"Your horse wants to jump." I didn't want him to think I was holding him back. "Why don't you go too?"

"Nah, Grant's just showing off, acting big in front of Hayley. I'll wait until cross country jumping's properly on the agenda."

Pleased he'd stayed with me, but wondering rather miserably about his obvious dislike of the dark-haired Grant, I couldn't think of the right thing to say, so again I stayed very quiet. We were riding at the rear of the line of horses, with June taking the lead followed by the two sisters plus Chas and Lee. June had relaxed now that we were back on home ground, letting her big gray mare, Celtic Lady, stretch her neck on a long rein while she chatted away to the group riding with her. Oliver and I were quite a long way detached from them and they obviously hadn't noticed the disappearing act of Hayley and Grant.

"Is that a clicking noise coming from Lincoln's off fore?" Oliver brought the bay to a halt and leaned down over his shoulder. "I hope he hasn't got a loose shoe, it – "

With a whooping yell and a crashing of overhead branches, Grant, on the farm's piebald horse, Pablo, came flying straight at us, soaring over a stile tucked

away in the nearby trees. Both Flint and Lincoln shied violently at the sudden, frightening noise and the more highly-strung Lincoln reared up as he veered sideways. Even if Oliver had been sitting straight he'd have had little chance of staying put, but, leaning forward as he was, he literally flew over Lincoln's head to land with a sickening thud several yards away. With a superhuman effort I managed to stay in the saddle, spinning Flint and leaning over to grab at Lincoln's reins as he galloped, panic stricken, by. As I did so Hayley appeared, clearing the stile easily as she arrived at the scene.

She took one look at Oliver, huddled in a frighteningly still heap on the ground and began screaming, "He's dead; you've killed him! Grant, you've killed Oliver!"

# Chapter Two

Talk about a drama queen! For one horrible moment when I heard what she was screaming I nearly fell off my own horse with fright, but then I saw Oliver was starting to sit up so I stayed put.

"He's OK, just winded." Grant didn't look the slightest bit sorry.

"Is Lincoln all right?" Oliver was a bit pale, but his deep blue eyes brightened when he saw I'd managed to grab the bay horse. "Thanks, Yasmine, you're a star. Just what the heck did you think you were doing?" This was directed at Grant, who was grinning insolently down at him.

"Oh, no, here comes Mom!" Hayley said, pointing. "She'll go ballistic when she hears about this."

"Don't tell her," Grant said immediately. "We can say Lincoln shied at something else and Oliver fell off."

Oliver glared at him. "This was your fault, and you know it."

"Sure, sorry pal, but you don't want to get Hayley in trouble with her Mother, now do you?"

"Please, Oliver." Hayley was looking nervously at her rapidly approaching mother.

Oliver sighed and brushed the dust off his sweater. "OK."

I was furious, feeling he was letting them off too lightly, but as usual I stayed silent.

June had reached us now, looking concerned. "Did I hear you scream, Hayley? What's happened?"

"Oliver fell off," Grant said smoothly "His horse shied at a rabbit or something."

"Lincoln veered sideways and reared at the same time." I just had to say *something*. "Oliver had no chance."

"You're not hurt, I take it?" June was frowning. "I hope your horse isn't going to be too nervous for this camp, 'cause we've got all sorts of things planned."

"He'll be fine," Oliver said shortly, taking Lincoln's reins from my fingers and remounting irritably. "I'm sure whatever spooked him was a one time deal, and won't happen again."

"That's right," Hayley put in eagerly "Sorry I screamed, Mom."

"Come on, then." June eyed us all doubtfully, thinking, I'm sure, that we weren't giving her the whole story. "The rest of our visitors arrive soon and I want to be there to greet them."

We trailed back, mostly staying quiet except for Hayley who chattered away in her usual style, seemingly forgetting the scare we'd just had. In the stable I gave Flint a good rub down and spent some time scratching behind his ears, which he loves.

"You can do me next." Oliver leaned over the stable door, giving me his fabulous grin.

"You probably need a bit of TLC after that fall." I smiled back, trying not to show I was annoyed he'd lied to save Hayley from trouble.

"I'm all right, but it could have been much worse. That moron Grant should be benched for dangerous riding, in my opinion."

"You should have stopped him," I said lightly, turning my back to give Flint a last cuddle.

"I know I should, but it seemed like a bad way to start this summer camp." He came into the stable and ran his hand along Flint's neck, touching my fingers as he did. "I didn't thank you properly for managing to catch Lincoln." He looked at me almost shyly. "I don't know how you did it, but you were brilliant. I'd have murdered those two clowns if he'd been hurt because of their stupidity."

I know it's petty, but I was pleased he was including Hayley in the blame. "It's OK, I'm glad I could do it." I didn't tell him my shoulder was really sore from being yanked nearly out of its socket by his panicking horse. "I'm going to turn Flint out in the paddock that June showed us. Is Lincoln going in there too?"

"Yeah, it'll do him good. Hold up – I'll get him and we can go together."

We took off our horses' head collars once we'd shut the field gate, and watched them canter off excitedly, Lincoln tossing his head and showing off to a small group of ponies in the adjoining paddock. We sat on the gate for a while, making sure they'd settle down.

"They look happy enough." Oliver hopped off the gate and put his hands around my waist to help me.

It was a lovely feeling, but I couldn't think of anything to say, so I didn't.

"You're very quiet,. Are you sure you're all right?" The deep blue eyes were on mine again and I wondered miserably if he was wishing I were more bubbly and vivacious, more like Hayley in fact.

"I'm fine." I hid behind my hair again. "Should we go and meet the rest of the crowd?"

It was a good evening. We had a delicious meal, and then spent the time playing silly get-to-know-you games.

"It's a different kind of game tomorrow." June beamed at us all. "Our first training session for the Black Horse Farm Mounted Games Competition."

I'd seen this on the schedule and was secretly delighted. Flint and I need a lot more schooling when it comes to jumping and dressage, but put us in the pony games and we're absolute demons! My bedroom wall at home is plastered with rosettes we've won, and I was really looking forward to being able to shine for once.

At first we were divided into groups, June instructing the riders who'd done very little in mounted games before while the rest of us, six in all, were with Terry, the summer camp's groom. We did a few practice runs of bending, where Flint's speed and flexibility made everyone gasp, the flag race, musical mats and a really funny dressing up race in which June had donated the most outlandish clothes I'd ever seen. Oliver was pretty good at all the games, though slightly hampered by Lincoln who tended to roll his eyes and step back from things like crazy hats and frilly bloomers! Grant seemed to find the whole thing way beneath his dignity, only attempting the bending on Pablo, who, as one of the summer camp's own ponies, was very good and obedient at everything.

Hayley was a scream, tearing around like a dervish on her chestnut mare, talking and laughing nonstop, but she was severely handicapped by not being able to vault back aboard Sika from the ground. Also, although her mare was really fast at the flag race, she refused to go back if Hayley missed one and was nearly impossible to pull up at the end. June came over to see how we were getting on. Terry, a heavy, balding man, hadn't said a lot, and just plodded around setting things up, but he pointed to me and told her, "The girl on the black pony's best."

"Well done, Yasmine, you'll be picking up a few rosettes at the end of the camp show, won't you?"

I smiled proudly, and Hayley said rather petulantly, "I'd have beaten her on my old pony, but Sika's too big and too flighty to help me."

"Told you so." June laughed at her daughter's pouting face and Oliver grinned at me, a look that seemed to draw the two of us together, almost like a couple.

Grant had dismounted and was leaning against a fence post, looking sullen. I couldn't help hearing June mutter to her daughter, "Why is he so bored? Hasn't Terry got him involved in the games?"

"Terry's hopeless, Mom." Hayley's voice was impatient. "I knew he'd be no good, and he's really lazy, always sneaking off somewhere when he should be working."

"Oh, dear." June looked worried. "I hoped he'd be able to help out, since your father's so busy, but it looks as though Dad's going to have to take over."

There were obviously problems with the running of the first summer camp, but I was sure June would get everything sorted out. She was a terrific teacher and organizer herself, lining us all up and getting everyone involved in the games. It was a terrific morning, and by lunchtime we'd all worked up a ravenous appetite. Maureen had prepared another great meal, and I saw June relax when she saw the laden table.

"Thank you so much," I heard her tell Maureen. "You're a real treasure. I thought with the way you tackled all the spring-cleaning when we moved in that we were lucky to have found you, but you're a wonderful cook too. I hardly have to spend any time in the kitchen."

"Thank you." Maureen placed the last dish of vegetables on the table. "I'll sort out that big cupboard under the stairs while you're riding this afternoon if you like."

"You're supposed to have afternoons free." June started serving our lunches. "Put your feet up and relax instead."

"No, I'd rather be doing something." She left the room as everyone descended like a pack of hungry wolves on the food.

The afternoon was going to be spent exploring the downs, and we chatted all through the meal, wondering what the horses' reactions would be to their first glimpse of the sea beyond. Everyone seemed to be enjoying themselves, and we were starting to get to

22

know each other. I didn't talk as much as most, but apart from having stabs of jealousy when Hayley flirted with Oliver, I was very happy. The blonde girl, looking cute as usual in a bright pink sweater, did most of the talking, and everyone seemed to like her vivid personality, including me – it was just that I hated the thought of Oliver liking her more than me! I was determined not to let my jealous thoughts spoil things and resolved to make more of an effort to make Hayley a friend. The trouble was trying to find a gap in her non-stop chattering, and when I did, I couldn't really think of anything mind-boggling to say.

In the end I pointed to a pendant she wore around her neck and said feebly "That's nice, Hayley, have you had it long?"

She grinned at me in her straightforward, cheerful way and said, "I actually found it the day we moved to Black Horse Farm, and although Mom doesn't agree, I think it's really valuable. She says it's just a piece of glass, but I think the red stone's a ruby, a fabulous jewel worth an absolute fortune!"

# Chapter Three

I'm afraid we were already so used to Hayley's dramatic over-the-top declarations that no one really responded. Because I'd started the conversation I made a show of examining the pendant. It was unusual, certainly, made of what looked like opaque glass in a cloudy blue-green color, and had an irregular oval shape with a wavy outline. Set just off center was the stone, bright red and sparkling, sure, but it was *tiny* so I couldn't help feeling June must be right and the pendant was just a piece of pretty, but worthless, glass.

After lunch when the horses had had time to digest their own midday feed, the whole crowd set off for our downs-exploring ride. I noticed Terry was left behind this time. Bill Preston, Hayley's dad, accompanied us instead. We all rode together at first, and I loved it, the fresh tang of the sea in the air, the beautiful contours of the downs beneath the horses' hoofs

25

and the excitement of our ponies being out in a group this big. I mostly ride on my own, so today was a whole new experience for both Flint and me. June was leading, and when we were all warmed up she set off along an upward sloping track at a brisk working canter, followed ecstatically by the twelve summer campers plus Hayley and Bill. It was all I could do to hold Flint; he went straight into racehorse mode again and kept trying to gallop past the ponies in front of us. Oliver was riding alongside me, laughing at my face as I did my best to keep my enthusiastic black pony under control at a medium canter pace.

"It's all right for you," I muttered between gritted teeth "Flint thinks this is play time and just wants to race."

Oliver laughed again and yelled back smugly, "I'm having no trouble with Lincoln; he's being really – "

There was a screech and Hayley, on a wildly galloping Sika, came thundering past, causing Lincoln to buck excitedly and try taking off behind her. Oliver nearly lost his seat again but managed to stay put and wrestle his bay horse back under control. Hayley was still flying ahead, and as she zoomed past the other horses nearly every one of them skittered and plunged into a gallop, turning the whole ride into a kind of mad cavalry charge. Despite her rider doing all the right things, sitting still, leaning back slightly and doing "give and take" aids with her reins, the naughty Sika was still bolting, now passing June on her stately gray mare. There seemed to be horses and ponies belting off in all directions with June and Bill trying to calm everyone down and regain control of the ride. Luckily no one fell off, though some of the less experienced riders looked as though they might at any time, and gradually we all managed to slow down enough to come to a ragged halt at the top of the track. We stood there, our horses' sides heaving as June did a rapid head count.

"Is everyone OK? What on earth was all that about? What started them all off?"

No one liked to say "Hayley" except Grant, who sneered and said, "It was Hayley. She just came bombing past Pablo and spooked all the other horses into racing with her."

"Hayley!" June sounded really mad, then realized her daughter wasn't amongst us. "Where *is* she?"

"I'm here, Mom." Hayley's voice was very subdued as she trotted back towards us on her sweat - soaked mare. "Sorry, I don't know what got into her. She just squealed suddenly and took off, and I couldn't stop her. I'm very sorry if I frightened any of you."

"I don't know about our visitors, but you sure scared the heck out of me." Bill glared at her crossly. "If you're not going to act responsibly, Hayley, you can just go back to the farm. Someone could have been hurt thanks to you."

"I'll go with you, Hayley," Grant said immediately, his face set in a sympathetic smile.

I couldn't believe my ears – only minutes before he'd blabbed that it was her fault the stampede had started! I looked uneasily at Oliver who was frowning as he stared at Grant. He opened his mouth to speak, but June cut in irritably.

"I don't want any of you going back. Hayley, you'll probably be less of a hazard with a smaller group. You and a couple of strong riders can keep a short distance in front of the rest of us."

"That's me, then." Grant immediately rode Pablo over to join Hayley, and she gave him a grateful little smile.

"We'll come too." Oliver was still giving Grant a hard look as he turned Lincoln away from the main group.

I stayed where I was, a very large jolt of jealousy and uncertainty rolling over me. Oliver seemed concerned for Hayley and obviously didn't want Grant to be alone with her. I was sure he'd think I was a nuisance if I tagged along too.

"Anyone else?" June asked brightly, pretending not to notice the lack of enthusiasm for joining Hayley and her manic mare.

"Come on, Yasmine." Oliver spoke quite irritably.

I walked Flint towards him, trying to appear very cool, and when I was near enough he hissed, "We can't leave her on her own with him. Grant's up to something."

I was tempted to rejoin the others, thinking resentfully that if he was so bothered he could work it out himself, but I'm just not the flouncing off type, I suppose. The four of us rode off at a respectable working trot until we'd put a few hundred yards between us and the larger group,

All of us, even Hayley, were silent at first, but then she burst out, "It's not fair! Mom and Dad are both mad at me because they think I can't control Sika."

Having just seen her carted off by the strongly pulling mare I silently agreed with her parents. Oliver, however, said, "She was really bolting back there. It looked as though she'd had a fright. Have you checked her over?"

"You think she might have hurt herself?" Hayley was instantly concerned. "She's not lame or anything, but now that you've said that, she did kind of leap forward as though she'd been stung."

"That'll be it," Grant said, looking even more sullen than usual. "You were just in front of me, and I saw Sika shoot sideways before she took off."

I thought it was mean of him not to have mentioned

that to June when he told her the fiasco was all Hayley's fault, but I didn't say anything. The atmosphere was already too tense to complicate it further. Although it was still a beautiful day, the glow had gone out of it for me. We rode across the rolling green curves of the downs, and even our first sight of a sparkling sea couldn't raise my spirits. Oliver was completely silent, keeping his eyes almost permanently fixed on Grant, who in turn, spoke only to Hayley, moving in very close and practically whispering in her ear. She, true to form, began to perk up with all this male attention and was soon back to her nonstop yammering. I hung back, probably looking sulky, but I just didn't want to be in the way if Oliver wanted to concentrate on the blonde girl. I couldn't understand why he'd called me to join them; he was certainly showing no interest in me now.

"Yasmine!"

I must have been so deep in self-pity I hadn't heard him.

"Come closer – what's the matter?" he was hissing crossly.

"Just enjoying the scenery," I lied, keeping my tone deliberately light.

"You don't say. Wish I could, but I have to keep an eye on Grant. He's definitely up to something, but I don't know what."

Grant was leaning across Pablo's shoulder to touch Hayley's hand; he'd be sitting behind her on Sika's saddle if he got any closer.

"I'd say it was some heavyweight flirting, wouldn't you?" I smiled as I said it, to show I wasn't bothered if Oliver was being made jealous by it.

"Flirting my – " He broke off. "Look, he's trying to get her away from us."

Grant was indeed increasing speed on Pablo, and his left hand was now holding Sika's reins so he'd take Hayley with him. Oliver immediately put Lincoln into a canter and caught up with them. I felt really stupid left on my own, and decided miserably that I'd give up my idea of getting to know Oliver better and spend this vacation alone. "Or with someone who isn't crazy about bubbly blondes," I thought resentfully. "There must be *someone,* surely!"

"Yasmine!" it was Oliver again, yelling now. "Come *on*!"

I tried to look not bothered as I approached and Oliver ran a hand over his good-looking face as if he couldn't believe my cool. Grant made a few more attempts to move Hayley away from us, but Oliver refused to cooperate and we ended up back on the farm, still together. The big group was just behind us, laughing and talking about the ride and what they'd seen, and I felt quite envious that they'd had such a good, uncomplicated, time. I gave myself a shake – what a whining little misery I was turning out to be!

There was another slight ruckus when we got back to the house after sorting out our ponies. Hayley, still huffy at what she saw as her parents' unfair treatment of her, had dashed upstairs for an early shower. We heard yet another shriek and June raised her eyes to heaven.

"What *is* the matter with that girl? Hayley, what are you screaming about now?"

Hayley appeared at the top of the stairs, wrapped in a fluffy pink towel. "Someone's just tried to steal my ruby pendant!"

"What do you mean?" her mother said impatiently.

"Just what I said. I was about to get in the shower when I realized I didn't have a clip to tie up my hair, so I went back into my room and saw a hand sliding around the door."

She did look quite shaken, I thought, and felt sorry no one was sympathizing.

"A hand – oh, for goodness' sake!" June said. "It was probably one of the guests opening the wrong door by mistake."

"No, they were definitely reaching for the necklace," Hayley said stubbornly. "I'd left it on the bedside table right next to the door, and that's exactly what the hand was going for."

"Nonsense." June turned away. "Hurry up – you should be helping out down here."

Poor Hayley stomped back into her room and reappeared in the kitchen shortly afterwards, hair still damp from the obviously hurried shower. I noticed she was wearing the pendant again and, feeling she'd been getting some pretty unfair treatment, said, "I'm glad they didn't get away with pinching the ruby."

Her face brightened immediately "Oh, thanks, Yasmine. I was beginning to think no one believed me."

"Believed what?" Oliver came over to join us and I instantly climbed back into my mental shell, assuming it was Hayley he wanted to talk to.

"We were wondering about the attempted theft." Hayley automatically batted her eyelashes at him.

He didn't seem impressed. "Like your mom said, probably a guest mistaking your door for theirs. It's a big old house, this, isn't it?"

"So?" She was clearly irritated. "We've only been here a couple of weeks ourselves, but I don't go around sneaking my hand into the wrong room. Anyway, if that's all it was, why did they run away?"

"Could it be that shriek of yours?" Oliver asked solemnly, reaching behind my back and giving my fingers a friendly squeeze. "That's quite a yell you've got there."

Hayley tossed her blonde curls and gave him a dirty look. "Yasmine believes me, don't you?"

I really did think something had scared her, so I said, "Yes. Maybe it would be a good idea to lock the pendant away somewhere safe."

"Why should I? I like it – it looks nice."

Oliver shrugged, clearly not bothered. "Suit yourself. Come on, Yasmine, the food smells good again. Will you sit with me?"

Hayley immediately went over to where Grant, Lee and Chas were listening to some music and we heard her going through the "hand round the door" story again.

"What is she like?" Oliver narrowed his eyes as Grant started moving very close to her. "You know, I just don't get what that creep is up to."

I wished he wouldn't touch my hand one minute, and then turn his attention to Hayley the next.

"Stay with her if you're so worried." I gave him my best false smile, cool and uncaring.

He looked at me. "I'd rather stay with you, but if I'm being a pain hanging around, just say so and I'll go."

He looked unhappy and I began to feel out of my depth and very confused. "You're not a pain. I – I just thought you'd prefer Hayley's company."

"Yeah, right. As if!" he said cryptically. "But I

think someone should be keeping a lookout for her. I don't know what Grant's up to, but I get the feeling she's not safe with him on her own."

I still felt his concern must mean he didn't want Grant and Hayley to get together, but he *had* said it, hadn't he? He'd actually said he'd rather be with me! I gave myself a hard mental shake and a good talking to. I was simply spoiling my own eagerly-anticipated vacation with all this negativity, and I resolved to control my jealousy of Hayley and get back on the warm, friendly basis that Oliver and I had started on our journey down to Black Horse Farm. It was quite an easy task that evening. We had a great time with Oliver and I teaming up for a Pony Quiz. We were so good together we actually won and received prizes of chocolate rosettes, presented very charmingly by Hayley. She'd soon gotten over her bad mood and thrown herself enthusiastically into the quiz, but she would yell out the first thing that came into her head, which was quite often wrong, and the evening ended with her being chased around the room by her team-mates who'd received the wooden spoon for worst result! Hayley didn't care. In fact she seemed to thoroughly enjoy all the attention, and we all went to bed in high spirits, laughing and talking as we looked forward to the next day.

# Chapter Four

I woke to glorious sunshine pouring through the window and leapt out of bed ready for action. After breakfast and the usual fun pony chores – I love bringing Flint in for grooming and tacking up, he's always so affectionate, rubbing his beautiful black head on my arm as if he's telling me he missed me – we were to set off on a different route, straight across the downs for our first dip in the sea. I couldn't wait. Flint loves water, and the thought of swimming through the waves with him was enough to make me burst into song.

"Oh, what a racket. You got a bad stomach ache, Yasmine?" Oliver peered over the door, grinning wickedly.

"Some people just don't appreciate fine music, do they, Flinty?" I chucked a dandy brush at his handsome blonde head and laughed when he pretended to fall down in a faint.

"What's going on?" Hayley sounded as cheerful as ever; her sulks and fears about the pendant obviously forgotten.

"Yasmine's beating me up." Oliver got back on his feet and I heard Grant say, rather sneeringly, "Pick on someone your own size, Oliver. You riding with me, Hayley? I'm ready to go."

"I've still got a bit of mud to scrape off Sika," Hayley said. "You go on, if you want."

"No, I'll wait for you." He was standing in the yard holding Pablo's reins and looking, I have to say, a bit large and menacing.

"Don't bother, Hayley's coming with us." Oliver was virtually squaring up to him. "We'll see you at the beach."

I could see Grant didn't like it. He hesitated, then swung into the saddle and gave Pablo a bad-tempered kick. "Suit yourself."

I had to work very hard to quell the instant surge of jealousy and insecurity, but I fought it down and soon we were riding out onto the beautiful contours of the downs, heading, this time, straight towards the sea. It didn't take long. A good warm-up of brisk walk and working trot, a nice pacey canter along a curving, up-hill path, and then we were dropping down again, picking our way carefully past the boulders and crevices of the cliff. Below us lay the beach, strewn with rocks at the cliff edge but widening into a broad stretch of golden sand. The sea, blue and sparkling, lapped against it, each gentle wave lace edged with creamy foam.

"Oh, how beautiful," I said, and Oliver turned to look at me.

I was talking about the view, of course, and felt myself blush deeply when, still looking straight into my face, he replied softly "Absolutely beautiful."

"Stop making eyes at each other, you two." Hayley, slithering expertly downhill on her big mare, was as loud as ever.

I saw Oliver give a resigned shrug and thought, slightly resentfully, that if he didn't like her tactless comments he shouldn't have insisted she ride with us again. I refused to let the thought spoil things, though, and eagerly joined in the ride along the sea edge, laughing at Flint as he lowered his head curiously to investigate this strange, ever moving expanse of water.

"Lincoln can't believe it either." Oliver brought his horse close. "He keeps stopping to blow through his nose at the waves."

We spent quite a while getting our ponies used to this phenomenon. Most of them, like Flint and Lincoln, were excited and interested, thoroughly enjoying themselves when we let them canter through the shallows, their hoofs kicking up great fountains of glittering spray. June was keeping a close watch on us all and told those she considered capable that we could change into swimsuits or shorts, remove our horses' saddles and take them in a bit deeper for a real swim. I couldn't wait, and raced back up the beach to change. The groom, Terry, looking more interested than usual, was to stay with the non-swimmers while June and Bill accompanied the rest of us. I quickly peeled off my T-shirt and riding pants, having already put my bathing suit on underneath.

"Yasmine, you're so lucky." Hayley was looking at me enviously "Really long legs and a great figure. I'm going to look like a garden gnome next to you."

"Don't be silly." I felt a bit shy and pulled the T-shirt back on.

"That's a good idea." She certainly did look very small. "I'll keep covered up too, and then maybe no one will notice what a midget I am."

We carefully stowed our boots, pants and stuff, along with the saddles, in the sheltered area of rocks. I vaulted easily onto Flint's bare back and held Sika, who was dancing with excitement, while Hayley scrambled onto a boulder so she could do the same. Once onboard she followed me back down the beach to join the other swimmers. I wasn't surprised to see that Jessica and Mandy, plus a couple of other less experienced riders, were going to stay out of the deep water, but everyone else seemed really keen and a lot of squealing and laughing went on as we rode the horses further into the sea.

It was just magical, the warmth of my pony beneath me, sensing every twitch of his muscles as he walked powerfully through the gentle waves. It was a weird sensation when the water reached my feet the first time, cool and silky against warm skin. Flint was surging strongly into deeper water as it rose higher and higher, touching his chest, then lapping against his shoulders. And then he was swimming, and I felt like a water nymph astride his beautiful sleek back, laughing with sheer joy as Oliver and Lincoln swam beside us. Two or three of the ponies weren't as keen, and we could see them standing stubbornly in the shallows, but the rest of us, with June and Bill keeping a careful watch, had the most wonderful time.

The only casualty was, inevitably, Hayley. Sika took a lot of convincing to get deep enough for her hoofs to leave the bottom, and when Hayley finally managed to push her forward, the flighty chestnut plunged so strongly that the waves she created knocked Hayley off the wet, slippery back. Hayley shrieked, of course, but kept hold of the reins, swimming alongside her mare's head until Sika was calm enough to let her rider back on board.

"It's like trying to ride a demented otter!" The

41

blonde girl was soaked through, and around her neck I could see the sparkle of the pendant, swinging out from underneath her T-shirt.

June was getting everyone to turn now, heading back toward the part of the beach we'd started from. Flint was funny again as we entered the shallow water, looking down at his legs as if he couldn't believe his hoofs were once again touching the ground. Lincoln came out of the water prancing and snorting like a stallion, with Oliver, looking incredibly gorgeous in just a pair of denim shorts, throwing his head back and laughing amidst the shower of spray that glittered like diamonds around him. It was one of those moments I wished I had a camera, but I knew it didn't matter. I'd always keep that picture in my mind to bring out and smile about whenever I chose. Jessica, Mandy and the others were waiting on the shore to greet us, looking a bit envious, I thought.

"That looked great," Mandy called to us. "We've been watching you, and we're definitely gonna try it next time."

There was a great hum of talking and laughing as we all made our way up the beach.

"Take turns holding each other's horses while you change back into your dry clothes." June and Bill both looked as though they'd enjoyed their dip as much as we had.

"Give me Flint and you can change first, Yasmine." Hayley grinned at me and I slid off my lovely boy's back, gave him a big hug and handed his reins to the blonde girl.

I toweled my legs really vigorously, not wanting to keep Hayley waiting too long. She, of course, was soaked from head to toe, her hair clinging to her face in tight wet curls, but she didn't seem to mind and chatted away in her usual cheerful fashion while I got back into my pants and boots. I hadn't brought a dry T-shirt, but the one I'd worn in the sea was only a bit wet, so I was soon hopping back over the rocks to take over Flint and Sika. Hayley, in turn, made her way to where she'd left her stuff, but when she reached her saddle she let out one of her piercing yells.

"What's the matter?" I turned my head, expecting to see her running away from a crab or something.

"My clothes are gone." She was hunting around in the rocks. "All of them, completely vanished!"

"You rolled them up and stuffed the bundle under your saddle," I reminded her, thinking privately she was proving to be a walking disaster.

"I know." She picked up Sika's saddle and peered underneath again, then did the same with Flint's, which was nearby. "Maybe my Mom or Dad moved them." She cupped her hands around her mouth and yelled, "Have you got my clothes, Mom?"

June, who was further along the beach, called back irritably, "Of course not. Stop shouting, Hayley."

"Oh, thanks a bunch!" Poor Hayley kept on searching.

I couldn't help because I had my hands full with the two horses, both of whom were showing signs of a great desire to roll in the sand, something I'd rather they didn't do until they were completely dry.

"What's up?" Oliver, covered up again in his riding clothes, (to my secret disappointment) wandered towards us.

"Hayley's lost her clothes," I said, and she immediately stopped hunting around and postured dramatically.

"They're not lost, they're *stolen*!"

"Who'd want to steal your stuff?" Oliver yawned, not showing any inclination to help.

I instantly felt sorry for Hayley and asked Oliver if he'd hang on to Flint and Sika while I gave a hand in the search.

He took the reins, giving my hands another squeeze and winking at me as he did so. I felt myself go all hot again and moved off quickly to help Hayley. She was now in the middle of the group, asking everyone if they'd seen her missing clothes. I went in the opposite direction, peering behind each rock without really expecting to see anything, but as I approached the big boulder that marked the path by which we'd ridden down to the beach, I saw a jodhpur boot, and then a pink sweatshirt.

"Over here!" I called, and Hayley sprinted along the beach to join me. The clothes had been dropped one by one, and I followed their trail, picking up a towel, another boot, and finally Hayley's navy blue riding pants.

"Here you go." I handed her the towel and started shaking sand out of the other stuff. "Someone's idea of a joke, I suppose."

"Very funny, ha, ha!" She scowled and rubbed her hair crossly. "Thanks, Yasmine."

"Everything all right, Hayley?" June was approaching, leading her horse. "Oh, you've found your clothes, have you? Hurry up and get dressed so you can dry Sika off."

"But Mom, someone took my stuff and dumped it over here. Some joker, Yasmine thinks, but I'm not so sure."

"Who else would it be?" June was busy doing as head count, making sure we were all present and accounted for.

"I don't know – yes I do!" Hayley put her hand theatrically to her throat. "The thief! The person who tried to steal my pendant last night – it must be him!"

# Chapter Five

"Don't be silly," her mother said dismissively. "A thief would have kept it, and not just dumped it behind a rock."

"But it wasn't with my clothes. I was wearing it when we went into the sea." Hayley lifted the pendant on its fine leather cord and flapped it up and down. "Wasn't I, Yasmine?"

"You were," I agreed, and June looked at me and raised her eyes to heaven.

"In which case Yasmine's first thought was right, and it was just someone's idea of a laugh."

"Maybe the thief didn't know I was wearing it. I had it tucked inside my T-shirt. " Hayley was in full flow but June turned away and started rubbing her horse down with an old towel, saying crossly, "Just get on with it, Hayley. I haven't got time to listen to your crackpot theories."

Oliver led Flint and Sika to us and handed their reins to me. "Here you are. I'd better finish drying Lincoln. Will you ride back with me, Yasmine?"

"Sure." I smiled, feeling a rush of happiness that he wanted me to be with him.

We had another great ride over the downs, taking a curving route, which took a little longer. Hayley was cantering ahead, accompanied by Lee and Chas and followed, I noticed, by a dour-looking Grant. Oliver seemed to keep his eye on the group but at first spent the whole time beside me, talking and laughing about our morning swim. The track led us through a small wood where trees had been felled and the logs stored in tall piles. We saw Hayley clear one of them, easily soaring into the air on her chestnut mare. I knew Oliver would jump it too, and wondered if he'd go off without me when he saw I wasn't going to try. I'd only done novice stuff, and without a ground line or cross poles to help me, wasn't at all sure about my ability to get Flint over without putting him at it all wrong. Or worse still, hurting him by jabbing his mouth.

Oliver, watching my face, said casually "I'll go first. You tuck Flint in behind us and follow."

*No way!* I thought, but then hesitated, looked into the warmth of his deep blue eyes and said, "OK."

Oliver put Lincoln into a nice controlled canter and

began approaching the log pile in a straight line. I could see by the bay horse's pricked ears and perfect outline that he knew what he was doing and loved it too. Flint and I bowled along behind them and I tried to sit quietly just like Oliver and remember everything I'd ever been told about impulsion and balance. There wasn't a lot of time; I saw Lincoln rise athletically, snapping back his forelegs to soar easily over the solid-looking jump. Flint followed, seeming to go up and up and UP, and then he was down again, cantering smoothly on the springy forest floor on the other side.

"Well done." Oliver turned his head and gave me his fabulous grin.

I was incredibly proud of my wonderful pony and burst into speech for once. "Wasn't Flint *great*! I've never tried anything that high – didn't have the confidence, I suppose, but that – that felt brilliant!"

"It was." Oliver laughed into my excited face. "And you're right, all you need is the confidence to take on more advanced schooling and you'll be competing in the same classes as me and Lincoln."

"D'you really think so?" I glowed.

"Absolutely. You've got the talent and so has your pony."

"Flint is just the best." I lay forward on my horse's neck and hugged him ecstatically.

"So you'll take your name off this afternoon's

novice jumping list and join us big boys in the advanced class? You're ready to move up, you know you are."

At that moment I felt Flint and I could take on the big wall in a Puissance contest, so I nodded happily. I'd been so involved with the big jump that while we were walking along I hadn't noticed that Hayley and the three others had almost disappeared from view. Oliver had, though, and he put Lincoln back into canter, seeming anxious to catch up with them again.

"Look!" He pointed ahead and I saw his mouth set in a grim line. "Grant's trying to get Hayley to leave Chas and Lee and ride off somewhere with him."

It was true; we were close enough now to see Grant moving Pablo very close to Sika, almost pushing the chestnut mare off the track.

"Oh, no you don't." Oliver asked for a gallop and we raced the few hundred yards to halt just behind Hayley and Grant.

"It's the lovebirds!" Hayley was irrepressible. "Hello, you two. I thought you'd sneaked off somewhere to be alone together."

"Funny you should say that." Oliver was unsmiling as he stared into Grant's face. "You looked as if you had the same idea."

"Oh, Grant just wanted me to try a different route from everyone else, but I told him I couldn't. Mom wants me to make sure no one gets lost, and I only know this way home so far."

"We won't get lost." Grant was returning Oliver's hard look. "And now that there's four of them in this bunch they'll easily find their own way back."

"But we want to stay with Hayley." Oliver didn't turn his head, "Don't we, Yasmine?"

"Yes," I said, feeling the by-now familiar sinking feeling.

He'd done it again; made me feel I was really special, and then ridden like a madman to prevent Grant from going off with Hayley. My fragile confidence ebbed away and I couldn't bear the thought that Oliver might just be acting kind to me; helping me out with my riding, while it was Hayley he really wanted. I hung back again and listened miserably as the blonde girl talked the whole way home, watching her as she flirted happily with all four males in turn. I decided, yet again, to give up, to leave the stage clear for her and Oliver to get together if that was what he wanted.

The jumping classes were due to start later in the afternoon, giving the ponies a good rest before they started work again. Before Oliver could confuse me any further I slipped away from everyone after lunch, taking a long walk across one of the farm's paddocks into the peace and quiet of the woods beyond. I was feeling miserable and sorry for myself, so when I heard the cracking of twigs behind me that meant someone was approaching, I slid behind the trunk of a huge, ancient oak tree and sat there, waiting for the other person to go on by.

"You look like a forest sprite, curled up amongst all this greenery." Oliver, his good-looking face slightly wary, sat down beside me. "Mind if I join you?"

"It's a free country." My voice sounded high and brittle, even to me.

He sighed and put his hand on my arm. "Yasmine, we have to talk. You're driving me nuts, giving out all these conflicting signals."

"I didn't know I was important enough to be signaling anything to you." To my dismay I could feel tears prickling behind my eyes and I turned my head away quickly.

He reached out and touched my chin gently, bringing me back to face him.

"Look," he said softly, "if I'm just making a fool of myself here, you've got to tell me. I – I really like you, and I thought you were starting to like me too."

"Of course I do." I'd nearly regained my composure and was trying to sound light and casual again. "I just don't want to get in your way, that's all."

"Get in my – " He looked genuinely baffled. "I don't get it."

"No, right." I wanted to get up and walk away, but he was still holding my arm. "Stop playing games, Oliver, it's not fair on me and it's not fair on Hayley either."

"Games? Hayley?" he tightened his grip and I winced. "I'm sorry." He let go immediately and I started to get up. "Don't go, please, Yasmine. I'm going crazy here. You're great with me one minute, and then back to being the Ice Maiden the next – what's that got to do with games or Hayley?"

I felt a sudden rush of temper. "You want me to spell it out, do you? OK, Oliver, if you're interested in Hayley that's fine with me, but don't try and string me along at the same time."

He stared at me for a second – then threw his head back and started laughing. I ducked away from him and started to run. It was too much. How could he mock me like this? I only managed about three steps before he grabbed me again and held me tight against his chest.

"Look, you idiot!" It was surprising how loving he made it sound. "It's not Hayley I'm after, it's *you*. You must know that."

"No, I don't." I looked into his face. "You're so jealous of Grant all the time that you want Hayley with you and not with him, and – "

He said a rude word and shook me gently. "I *don't*

53

want her to be with me, but you're right, I have been trying to keep Grant away from her."

"Why?" As you can tell, I'd given up my cool act.

He shuffled his feet and looked embarrassed. "It sounds a bit soft, but I'm really sorry for her. I've got a kid sister who's a total pain just like Hayley, but as well as me, she's got my Mom and Dad looking out for her. Hayley's parents are so wrapped up in getting this summer camp business off the ground they're not taking any notice of her at all."

"That's true," I admitted. "But surely it's OK for Grant to like Hayley?"

"I'm not at all sure he does." Oliver had put his arm around my waist and it felt great. "He's much older, for a start. I just don't believe he's only fifteen. Why would a guy like him be after a maddening little kid like Hayley?"

"Why else would he keep trying to get her alone?" I tried to concentrate as we walked through the dappled shade beneath the trees.

"*I* don't know." He stopped, his arm still around me. "But now that we've sorted things out between us, we could find out, become a kind of detective couple."

I liked the idea of being any kind of couple with him. "OK." I let my hair slide forward. "But only if you really want to be with me."

He put both hands up and cupped my face, brushing the long hair gently back. "I do."

"OK," I said again and wondered how to stop the incredible gymnastics my heart seemed to be doing. To calm down I tried to think about being a "detective." "You don't – you don't suppose Hayley's right, and someone really is after that pendant she found? It could have been Grant trying to steal it last night and the pendant is the reason he's trying to get her alone."

"Maybe, though it couldn't have been him today, could it? He was in the sea with us when Hayley's stuff was taken," Oliver pointed out. "Anyway, I can't believe anyone would be trying to steal the thing, it's just a cheap old thing."

"It does look like glass," I agreed. "But if it *is* valuable it could be what Grant's after."

"It was found in the house just after Hayley's family moved in. Let's find out a bit of Black Horse Farm's background. There must be local people who know the history of the place."

"Maybe a fabulous jewel went missing in the olden days." I smiled at him, feeling great but still a bit shy.

"And it's turned up disguised as Hayley's pendant – yeah, right!"

"But like you said, it *was* found in the house. That could be significant." I was still trying hard to think

about the pendant and not get too excited about the warmth in his eyes every time he looked at me.

"OK." His hand went around my waist. "We've got some free time tomorrow. Want to go into town and see what we can find out?"

We left the woods and started walking back across the paddock. The only time he took his arm from around me was when we stopped to make a fuss over Flint and Lincoln. It was wonderful, standing with Oliver in the sunlit meadow, breathing in the scent of my beautiful black pony and looking forward in a lighthearted way to becoming a "detective couple" with him. I had no idea then, of course, that there really *was* a mystery at Black Horse Farm – a mystery that would give us a lot of trouble before we were able to solve it.

# Chapter Six

I started to realize something serious was going on later that evening. The afternoon had been good after a shaky start. I'd trotted Flint across to the schooling ring where the advanced jumping class was being held, feeling sick with nerves. This made my pony jittery, of course, and he began jogging uneasily and shaking his head about.

"Relax!" Oliver commanded, giving me a great grin as he said it. "You're tensed up like a coiled spring. Poor Flint's wondering where his usual calm rider has gone."

I made a huge effort and eased out my bunched-up muscles and the stiffness in my joints. Flint immediately settled down and Oliver blew me a kiss, only half jokingly, I think.

"That's better," he said. "When June comes in to start the lesson she'll want us all to warm up first so – oh, no!"

I turned to see what had prompted the dismay in his voice and felt like groaning too as Terry made his way into the center of the school. He was a rotten teacher, disorganized and with no enthusiasm or, it seemed to me, half the know-how Oliver had demonstrated. We had a lack-luster twenty minutes or so of walking and trotting in circles, and then Terry dragged a few poles around and said we could try a course.

"What, no lateral work to encourage suppleness, no basic dressage moves to get the horses' attention?" Oliver grumbled under his breath. "Come on, Yasmine, you and I can do our own thing in one of the corners. You're not going to learn anything with Terry."

I thought it was really sweet of him to spend his time concentrating on my schooling and enjoyed the next half hour or so very much. Flint and I worked hard, but the improvement I felt every time we jumped made it so worthwhile. June arrived, cheerful and friendly as ever, but her face fell when she walked into the ring. It was a shambles, with Lee and Hayley squabbling over the correct distance to set up their jumps, Chas ambling around haphazardly, and a bored-looking Grant sitting on the ground, legs stuck out in front of him as he listened to the Walkman strapped to his ears.

"How is the class going, Terry?" June asked

sharply. "I presume this is a break in the organized session?"

"Something like that." The man didn't seem bothered. "I'll have a coffee break now, if you're taking over."

She watched him slouch over to the farmhouse, and could barely suppress her annoyance. "Sorry, guys, if you haven't had much of a lesson so far."

We all smiled and said it was OK, but could quite clearly hear the anger in her voice when she asked Hayley what the group had done so far.

"Nothing, really. I told you Terry's no good, Mom. You can't use him for teaching."

"He said he had loads of experience, and I thought he was going to turn out to be a gem, like Maureen. Though having said that, she seems to have her downside as well. It was all she could do to get breakfast ready this morning. I don't know what's come over her."

I felt sorry for June. She was trying so hard to make the summer camp a really fabulous experience for all the young riders, and it was getting off to a rocky start with all these staff problems. Still, I had no complaints. Now that Oliver and I had sorted ourselves out, I was having the best time EVER. We had a good schooling session with June, and I gave Flint about a million hugs and kisses before I turned him out for the night.

"You were wonderful," I whispered in his ear, and he nudged me affectionately as if he agreed completely.

Oliver and I watched our two horses trot happily into their field, and although we groaned when they lay down and rolled ecstatically in the dustiest patch they could find, we didn't begrudge them. They'd both worked hard enough to deserve some fun.

June and Bill, obviously deciding their visitors were also in line for some entertainment, set up a rip-roaring evening of games again. The sky outside was black by the time someone suggested we end the day with a mind-tingling game of "Murder in the Dark." It's a creepy game where you pick cards to secretly select who's going to be the victim and the murderer, and then after the lights go out and the murder is committed, the victim is found "dead" on the floor and you have to discover the identity of the killer.

I find it quite spooky and can never think of any relevant questions to help with the detecting. Still, I welcomed the idea tonight, since it would give Oliver and me a taste of being a detective couple. The cards were selected, everyone began wandering around the great hall and the living room, and then suddenly the main switch was hit and the whole house plunged into darkness. I didn't know if Oliver had picked the murderer's card or not, but I took a chance and clung onto

61

his hand anyway, feeling a lot braver with the comforting touch of his fingers. There was a lot of suppressed giggling and the odd squeak as people bumped into furniture or each other in the pitch black, and then – from the next room a fearful, ear-piercing scream, followed by a horrible choking sort of shout, echoed 'round the lofty hall. For a few minutes it was pandemonium. Whoever was supposed to press the main switch back on didn't, and we all stumbled clumsily about, apologizing every time we trod on a toe or stuck an elbow in someone's ribs.

"Lights!" called out June's voice. "Come on – *lights*!"

At last someone found the switch, and lights blazed all over the house. We all blinked, and then looked around for the "victim's" body. No one was lying on the floor, but there, leaning against the hall door, was Hayley, her hair all tousled and her face very white.
"Some – somebody tried to strangle me," she said in a choking, but being Hayley, dramatic way.

"You're supposed to lie down and you're supposed to be dead," June said crossly.

"I'm – I'm not playing the game." The blonde girl sounded so upset I quickly ran over to her.

"Look!" She put a hand to her throat, and to my horror I saw a thin red line where something had dug into her skin.

"She's hurt." I turned to June, and she rushed over and inspected her daughter's neck quickly.

"Oh, that's nasty. Someone's playing much too rough. Who was the murderer?"

"Me." Lee stepped forward and held up the card. "But I didn't touch Hayley, I promise. I hadn't managed to do my murder yet, and anyway, she wasn't the victim I was going for."

Everyone gasped and crowded around poor Hayley.

"What made that mark?" Oliver asked her, pointing to the line on her neck.

"The leather cord of my pendant." She was nearly crying. "Someone grabbed me from behind and tried to tug it off me. It's too short to go over my head, so they were trying to break the leather, I think, and it dug into my throat and it really, really hurt."

Her mother put her arms around her and hugged her, but when she said, "Don't be silly, honey, you're obsessed with that silly pendant. It was just some nasty person's idea of a joke again." Hayley pushed her away and burst into tears.

"It's not a joke! Why won't you believe me?"

I hugged her instead. She was desperately upset and I couldn't understand June not taking the awful episode seriously. Although most of the other campers seemed to think June was right and Hayley was being theatrical again, it put a real damper on the

63

evening, and we all drifted off to bed feeling deflated. I did my best to bolster Hayley, offering to take the pendant and hide it in my room to stop whoever was after it, but she shook her head stubbornly.

"Mom's already told me to lock it away so I can't blame it for any more trouble, but I don't see why I should."

"But if you're right and they *are* after the pendant – " I began, but she pulled angrily away from me.

"*If* I'm right – I thought you believed me, but you're as bad as all the others, just thinking I'm making it all up!" she said.

"No I don't, honestly I – "But she was gone, flouncing upstairs and slamming her bedroom door so hard it shook.

"She'll get over it." Oliver obviously wasn't as sympathetic as I.

"But it was an awful experience for her." I was annoyed with him. "Whether it was a thief trying to steal the necklace or some idiot pretending to strangle her for a joke, it must have scared her to death."

"Not a great expression to use," Oliver said, grinning slightly. "Given we were playing 'Murder' at the time."

"Honestly, I give up. What's the matter with you all? Even her parents aren't taking it seriously!"

"Well, Hayley's such a drama queen, isn't she? I'm

sure she *was* scared, but she makes such a scene about everything. Don't be mad at me, Yasmine, I promise I'll try to find out what's going on."

I was sure that, like June and all the others, he thought the incident was just someone overdoing when playing a trick on Hayley, but by now I was convinced none of the strange things happening to the girl were meant as a joke. Still, Oliver was true to his word, and the next day, after a great morning of show jumping and dressage with June, we joined the group headed into town in the summer camp minivan. Hayley wasn't coming with us, but when we checked and found she was going to be with her parents, we thought it safe to leave her.

"Grant's gone off somewhere with Lee and Chas," I told Oliver. "So he won't be hanging around Hayley while we're gone."

He looked at me and pulled my long hair, gently mocking. "So you agree that Grant's probably up to no good?"

"Yes." I hesitated. "I thought he was suspiciously quiet last night after Hayley got hurt, and I can't help thinking he was the one trying to steal the pendant."

"I don't know about that." Oliver, unlike me, still didn't believe anyone would be after the *ruby*. "But I'm glad he's going to be out of the way while we're in town."

It was only half an hour's drive, and when we arrived the others in the van immediately rushed off to the shops or amusement arcades while Oliver and I, after studying a street plan, set off for the library. We didn't really know where to look or exactly what we were looking for, so we wasted ages wandering around the section with local history books.

"Nothing's exactly leaping out at me." Oliver peered over the top of a big tome and crossed his eyes at me.

I laughed (quietly, it being a library) and said, "Me neither. Black Horse Farm doesn't seem to feature that much. Maybe we should be looking at something more recent, like the local newspaper."

"Brilliant!" He put the book back on its shelf and pretended to salute me. "I can see you're gonna be a natural at detecting."

I gave him a friendly shove and we went off to find where the newspaper archives were kept. It didn't take long; a few years back the town's *Clarion* had given the story front-page headlines.

"Look!" I grabbed Oliver's arm and he immediately slid it around my waist, moving in very close to read what I'd found.

"*Black Horse Farm in Search for Missing Haul*. Wow, this must be it. Does it mention the pendant?"

"No." I'd been scanning the lines quickly and

shook my head. "It seems that the farm was owned by a man who masterminded a massive bank robbery. They've caught him, and there's a report on his trial."

"He was given fifteen years in jail, but he won't tell the police where he hid the money." Oliver's lips were so close I could feel his breath on my face. "Obviously the first place to be searched was Black Horse Farm, but despite virtually taking the place apart the stash of unmarked bank notes wasn't found."

"So where does the pendant come in?" I frowned; it was hard to think clearly with Oliver that near. "D'you think the robber bought it with the money he stole?"

"You're talking thousands and thousands of dollars," he said, sounding skeptical. "I can't believe that tiny little stone would cost all that."

"Maybe it's the stuff around it," I said excitedly. "It looks like glass to us, but it could be – oh, I don't know – precious jade or something."

Oliver turned his good looking face towards me, brushing my cheek briefly with his lips. "You think so?"

I gulped and moved back slightly, feeling a strange mixture of elation and shyness. "What else could it be? I know you don't believe Hayley, but she's convinced someone is trying to steal the necklace."

"And it all started happening immediately after she

told us she'd found the thing in the house when they moved in," he agreed, looking thoughtful (and gorgeous). "If you're right Hayley's in great danger, isn't she? June was annoyed when she thought someone was playing a trick that got too rough last night, but if there's someone at Black Horse Farm who knows the pendant is incredibly valuable, then both she and Bill should be told there's a real villain making a real attempt to steal it."

"I know, and now that Hayley's announced she won't ever take it off he's just going to use brute force to get it." I felt really worried. "Quick, we'd better get back to the farm to warn her."

"She won't take any notice," Oliver said gloomily "She's just like my sister, stubborn as a mule. She thinks that by wearing it all the time she'll stop the thief."

"And you don't believe that's true?"

"You only have to look at last night. It seems as though he'll stop at nothing to get that pendant from around her silly little neck."

# Chapter Seven

"That's a bit harsh." It was amazing, I thought. A few hours ago I was feeling really miserable that Oliver preferred the blonde girl, and now here I was telling him to be nicer about her! "It's not Hayley's fault there's a thief after the necklace."

"She's the one who insists on wearing it all the time," Oliver reminded me.

"Well OK, but it's the guy trying to steal it who's the criminal," I replied with spirit. "And we need to find him pretty quick. It's someone who can get into the house easily – have you noticed anyone skulking around?"

He looked at me as if I was mad. "Oh come on, you're kidding, aren't you? It's obvious who tried sneaking the ruby from her room, and you said yourself he went very quiet after last night's fiasco.

Probably really ticked off that he didn't manage to break that leather cord."

I stared at him. "Grant? You think the thief is Grant? But he's – he's only a little older than us."

"He's at least seventeen, in my opinion, and I said from the start there was no way he was following Hayley around because he liked her. It's the pendant he wants, not the girl."

I thought hard. "I'm not convinced. He was already paying her a lot of attention when we first arrived here, remember? At that time no one knew about the pendant being found in the house – oh yeah, and also –" I was getting quite fired up. "Grant couldn't have taken Hayley's stuff on the beach. We know he was in the sea with us."

"He could have sneaked back while we weren't looking," Oliver argued. "We were all so intent on swimming with the horses that no one would have noticed if he wasn't with us the whole time."

"June and Bill would." I could be pretty stubborn myself. "They were watching us all like hawks."

"Only from a safety point of view, and they were looking seawards for that. If Grant took longer than the rest of us to get into the water they'd think nothing of it."

"I s'pose so," I said reluctantly. "It's not that I like Grant particularly, he's too moody, but I hate the

71

thought that he's capable of hurting Hayley just to get the pendant."

"Judging by last night he's willing to hurt her quite a lot," Oliver said grimly. "The sooner we get back and make sure she's safe the better."

We had to hang around for the rest of the campers to get back to the van, and by the time we arrived at Black Horse Farm again I was wriggling around in my seat in nervous anticipation.

"Stop worrying." Oliver squeezed my hand gently. "Hopefully she's still with her parents. Grant won't dare try anything while they're around."

"But he might have tricked her into going off alone with him."

We'd already agreed that, without proof, we could hardly denounce Grant as a would be criminal, and I'd told Oliver he'd simply have to spend all his time guarding Hayley 'til we could catch Grant red-handed. To my relief, although the blonde girl was in the stable yard pushing a wheelbarrow around, there was no sign of Grant, or anyone else for that matter. Oliver and I quickly changed back into our horsy clothes and joined her in the yard.

"Like some help?" He really is fabulous when he smiles like that, and Hayley perked up immediately.

"Great, thanks," She said.

After that we didn't leave her alone for a minute,

and she really enjoyed the attention, batting her eye-lashes and flirting with Oliver every other minute. Now that I knew how he felt about me I didn't mind at all, and it was worth it to see that she was kept safe. Grant arrived in time for dinner, along with Chas and Lee, but he disappeared, presumably to his room, afterwards, and we had a much more relaxing evening without having to watch his every move. The next item on the summer camp schedule was a treasure hunt (on horseback, of course) and the next day Oliver and I had to fight hard to get into the group containing Hayley and Grant.

"But Yasmine," June said patiently, "we've worked it all out, you and Oliver are to join Jake and Tania. They're good riders, nearly the same level as you, and Bill will be leading. Hayley can stay out of trouble at the rear of Terry's group."

"The – um – the horses all know each other," I said lamely. "Flint and Lincoln like going out with Sika and Pablo, don't they Oliver?"

"Yes," he agreed, looking innocently at June's slightly irritated face.

She sighed. "OK. I thought you'd both like a break from my daughter and her nutty mare, but if you're so keen I'll ask Lee and Chas to swap groups."

The two boys, amiable as always, agreed, and we set off at five-minute intervals to follow the "treasure trail," each leader holding a printed sheet of instructions. It was good fun, following each clue across the glorious countryside. Although I didn't forget to keep Hayley in sight at all times, I thoroughly enjoyed cantering alongside Oliver as he sat easily on his bay horse. To my surprise Terry led us through the woods where the cross-country jumps had been built but, using Lincoln as a lead, Flint and I sailed over them all in great style. Hayley nearly came to grief when reaching out to pick a particular kind of leaf needed for the treasure hunt. She had to make a wild grab at Sika's mane when the highly-strung chestnut shied dramatically at a paper bag flapping in the hedgerow.

"Behave yourself, you lunatic!" Hayley pretended to clip her mare's ears as she wriggled back into the saddle and regained her stirrups.

I saw Grant glance quickly at her from under lowered black brows, but he made no comment. In fact, to our bewilderment, he seemed to take no interest in Hayley at all, merely riding in sullen silence behind Terry, who, as usual, only spoke when he absolutely had to. The route for the 'hunt' was a winding, circuitous one, leading us onto the track at the base of the downs one minute, then snaking back through the woods surrounding the farm house the next. We'd been the last group to leave and though at first we'd catch a glimpse of the others up ahead we were mostly alone, following the trail along which the clues led us. I'd relaxed a lot. Grant was making no attempt to get near Hayley, it was a beautiful day in wonderful surroundings, and I had Flint and Oliver for company, so it was – well, just heaven. A heaven made a bit noisy by Hayley, of course, who chattered and sang and asked questions the whole time. We'd dismounted to search around in a corner of the meadow for a special stone under which the next clue was hidden, when Terry's cell phone started ringing.

He listened briefly, and then said, "It's your mother, Hayley. She wants you over by the old wood shed to help with something."

"Oh no, let me speak to her." Hayley held out her hand for the phone.

"The reception's breaking up." He shook it and held it to his ear again. "It was faint just now, but I can't hear her at all any more."

"You've probably let the battery go dead." She had a poor opinion of Terry at all times. "I s'pose I'll have to go and see what she wants. I wouldn't help before because she didn't believe me about the pendant, and now she's paying me back."

"I shouldn't think that's true," I said, hoping to smooth things out between mother and daughter. "Go and help her – it probably won't take long."

"I'll go with you, Hayley." Grant spoke suddenly, and I could see Oliver tense up immediately.

"No, I'll go," he said, glaring at Grant.

Hayley beamed and simpered a bit, but Terry, still poking around in the grass with his stick, looked up and growled, "You can both stay and find this clue or we'll never finish this treasure hunt. Hayley, you get a move on or your Mom will give me another ear bashing."

I could see Hayley didn't like his tone, but after a slight hesitation she sprang back into the saddle and cantered off through the meadow, disappearing from view into the woods beyond. I watched her go, biting my lip a little, and then led Flint over to Oliver.

He saw I was worrying and whispered in my ear, "It's OK, she'll be fine as long as we keep Grant with us all the time."

I supposed he must be right, though I still found it hard to believe even the bad-tempered Grant would hurt the blonde girl to get at the pendant. The four of us hunted around in the long grass of the meadow, parting its feathery strands to find the stone hiding the next clue. So far we'd been pretty quick at unearthing each one but this time it seemed to take ages. The horses got quite bored and started snatching up mouthfuls of grass to munch while Terry and Grant searched one patch and Oliver and I scrabbled around in another, keeping a close eye on Grant while we worked. I started wondering why Hayley was taking so long, and just as I opened my mouth to say so, Terry suddenly gave a grunt of satisfaction.

"Found it. We'd better get going."

"What about Hayley?" I asked. "She won't know where we've gone."

"Tough." He swung heavily back into his saddle. "Though we'd better go and tell her, I guess, or she'll have something else to complain to her mother about."

I was glad he seemed scared of upsetting June, and thought if Hayley didn't complain about him I would! We followed him (he was riding one of the farm's steady old cobs) out of the sunlit meadow and entered the cool depths of the wood beyond. It was much darker here, with the canopy of leaves from the thick growth of beech and oak trees keeping out most of the sun. It was quiet too, with just an occasional burst of bird song and the soft thud of our horses' hoofs, muffled by the deep covering of dead leaves. It was probably the sudden chill and marked contrast from the bright countryside we'd just left, but I remember shivering nervously and feeling goosebumps standing out on my bare arms.

"Where are we going, Terry?" Grant spoke almost for the first time and the groom turned, the usual dour expression on his face as he replied "Only a bit further. June said she'd meet Hayley by an old wood shed that's up ahead somewhere."

"I wonder why?" Oliver was looking puzzled. "What did June want Hayley to help her with?"

"Don't ask me." The man shrugged, and then froze suddenly, looking through the trees. "There's something up there, look."

He kicked the cob on and we followed him along a narrow track that twisted its way between the great tree trunks. Suddenly the groom leapt out of the saddle and ran forward. We still couldn't see what he'd spotted so Grant, Oliver and I stood up in our stirrups to look, and I gasped at the scene before us.

"It's Hayley!" My voice came out in a croak as I saw the slim figure lying face down on the soft forest floor.

Her arms, in the unmistakable bright pink sweater she liked to wear, were flung wide, her blonde curls were tousled and she lay completely, utterly, and frighteningly still.

# Chapter Eight

Terry knelt at her side, turning her head gently to face him.

"It's OK, she's breathing," he said to our relief. "But she's unconscious and I can't move her in case anything's broken. Darn this phone, I can't call anyone to help. Grant, you'll have to ride to the house and call an ambulance. Wait for it, and then lead them back here, or as near as they can get."

"What can I do?" Oliver, like me, looked almost frozen with shock. "I know some first aid – "

"It's all right, it's best not to crowd her. I'll stay until the paramedics arrive. The best thing you can do is find Sika. Hayley's obviously taken a bad tumble, and the horse will be in a real panic."

"I'll get June, OK?" I started turning Flint away as Terry nodded.

"Good idea. Don't frighten her. Hayley's tougher than she looks, and I'm sure she'll be OK."

He seemed to have the situation well under control, I thought, watching him remove his jacket and place it carefully over the slight form of the blonde girl.

"Get going!" he growled impatiently. "See if you can find that stupid horse before she damages herself as well as Hayley."

We turned away quickly and began cantering through the woods, reining our ponies in and out of the closely-packed trees. It wasn't long before we reached the edge and were back again in the bright, sunlit meadow and in sight of Black Horse Farm. I guessed June, who must have left her daughter per-fectly well and safe in the woods, had rejoined her group of treasure hunters and was now further away on the downs track where the last clue would have led them.

"I'll go that way and fine June." I turned to Oliver. "What should I say – that Hayley's had a fall and is unconscious – or will that scare her too much?"

"Shouldn't think so. We all hit the ground from time to time, and it's usually not too serious."

"I think this fall is worse because Hayley's hat had come off and she must have banged her head." I was still worrying; the blonde girl had stayed so frighten-ingly still.

"Yeah, I noticed that too." He frowned, and then put Lincoln back into a canter. "I'm going to check the yard first. Sika would be most likely to head for home."

Flint and I galloped off in the opposite direction, hoping we'd soon see June and her group. In fact it was a good ten minutes before I spotted them ahead of me on the twisty track at the base of the downs. I obviously didn't want to go charging towards them screaming out the news of Hayley's fall, and I hoped my expression would show the right amount of concern but not panic. It had been a real shock seeing Hayley lying there like that, and of course my first thought had been that the would-be thief had attacked her. I didn't say any of that to June, but just called her name and trotted briskly to join her.

"Hayley's had a fall," I began, and her smiling face turned immediately to a grimace as she said, "That girl! It's just one thing after another with her!"

It wasn't quite the reaction I'd been expecting, and I forgot about being diplomatic.

"She's unconscious. Terry's stayed with her while Grant and Oliver have gone to call an ambulance and find Sika."

"Unconscious?" June went very pale. "Oh, poor Hayley! I knew I shouldn't have let her buy that untrustworthy mare. Where is she?"

"In the woods, over there." I pointed in what I thought was the vague direction and she frowned and shook her head.

"Where?"

"The woods where the wood shed is," I said, slightly impatiently.

"What was she doing in there? It's not part of the treasure hunt." June was already heading back towards the woods.

"She went there to meet you." I was starting to feel something was wrong again. "You know, after your phone call."

"I haven't made any phone calls." June increased the pace to a brisk working canter. "We'll sort that out later, Yasmine. You ride ahead as fast as you can and show me where my daughter is."

I could hear nervous squeaks of excitement as the five slightly timid girls in June's group tried to keep up with Flint's flat-out gallop across the meadow. I slowed down well before we reached the wood, not wanting the less experienced riders to go crashing headlong into any trees. It didn't take long to wind our way to the little clearing where Hayley still lay under Terry's jacket. To my unspeakable relief she was conscious now, though her face was chalk white and, unheard of for Hayley, she was completely silent.

"Honey!" June practically threw herself off Celtic Lady's back.

"Better not move her," Terry warned, "I don't think anything's broken, but you never know."

"How did it happen? I suppose Sika spooked and you fell off– oh, where's your hat?"

"I didn't fall." It was barely a whisper. "Someone came up behind me and hit the back of my head."

"Someone – Hayley, hon, don't be silly. Why would – "

"I'm *not* silly!" Tears filled her blue eyes. "They hit me so they could try and steal the ruby pendant again, and this time they succeeded. It's gone, Mom. They must have taken it off me after they knocked me out."

I felt a shudder run through me. I'd been dreading this, the confirmation of my first fear when I saw Hayley lying so still on the ground.

"Who saw what happened?" June stood up and looked distractedly at Terry. "She wasn't alone, I take it?"

"I'm afraid she was," I said, near to tears myself. "We thought it was all right because you'd phoned and told her to meet you."

"I most certainly did – " June began then broke off as Grant came riding towards us.

"The ambulance is just back there and the paramedics say they'll stretcher Hayley over to it." He looked genuinely upset, and I felt guilty when I thought how sure Oliver and I had been that he was the would-be pendant thief.

There was no question of that now, of course. We'd kept Grant firmly in our sight from the moment Hayley cantered out of the meadow until the dreadful discovery of her unconscious body. Now wasn't the time to be asking questions, though. The most important thing was to get Hayley the medical attention she needed. The paramedics were great, very quick and efficient; they soon had her strapped to a stretcher and into the ambulance. I felt a great deal better about her when I saw that Hayley, though still pale and fragile looking, was actually managing a little flirting with the young, good looking paramedic! June handed me Celtic Lady's reins as she climbed into the back of the ambulance.

"Turn my horse out for me please, Yasmine. Terry, get hold of Bill and explain what's happened. He can drive down to the hospital once he's sorted out all our visitors."

"Right." Always a man of few words, Terry remounted the patiently waiting cob and started riding away.

I called to Mandy and Jessica and the other three girls in June's group to follow me as I led the gray Celtic Lady out of the woods. It was a relief to leave the oppressive gloom of the woods and ride once more into warm, welcoming sunshine. We were all pretty subdued after what had happened to Hayley, of course, but the other five didn't know the full story and, unlike me, weren't blaming themselves for letting the blonde girl ride off on her own. I told Oliver how I felt when we met up again in the stable yard.

"Don't say that, Yasmine." He held my shoulders and shook me gently. "If it's anyone's fault it's mine. It was me who said she'd be OK as long as Grant wasn't with her, and I was wrong. All we can do now is hope Hayley makes a full recovery and in the meantime track down whoever it was who hit her. Stealing's bad enough, but to attack a little girl like that is – is – "

"Evil?" I suggested, and he nodded.

"If it's someone from the summer camp it shouldn't be hard to work out who had the opportunity." He'd obviously been doing a lot of thinking while he settled the unharmed Sika in her box.

"You think so?" I wasn't so sure. "Everyone was scattered all over the place. The only people we can definitely rule out are Terry and Grant."

"True, but the others were all in groups like us. We can question them all and see who had the chance to sneak off and thump poor Hayley. Did they hit her while she was riding, do you think, or had she dismounted for some reason?"

"I don't know. If she has to stay in the hospital I want to visit her and tell her we're on the case. I can ask her for all the details then and let her know her beloved Sika is safe, of course."

"Good idea. I can start with Terry, I suppose - ask him about that phone call June says she definitely didn't make."

"He said at the time it was a bad line and he couldn't hear her very well," I remembered. "So I suppose it could have been anyone, even a male voice pitched high."

"Someone put a lot of thought into planning this," Oliver agreed as we led our ponies back to their field. "It's going to be hard finding out just who."

We got straight to it, Bill kindly agreed to let me accompany him to the hospital, while Oliver, armed with notebook and pen, started "interviewing" all the other campers. Bill was obviously concerned about his daughter's injury, but hadn't really understood the significance of what she'd told us.

"Don't look so worried, Yasmine. Hayley's had falls before, and she'll be all right," he said as we drove towards town.

"But it wasn't a fall. Someone hit her." I knew he must have been told this, and was quite taken aback when he said easily, "Oh she's just dramatizing, as usual. She probably went too fast through the trees and knocked her head on a branch."

"What about the phone call?" I pointed out. "June didn't call and ask Hayley to meet her, but *someone* did. And the ruby pendant was taken from around her neck while she was unconscious."

"Are you sure?" He frowned and looked worried at last.

"Quite sure. I want to see if Hayley's OK, of course, but the other reason I'm coming with you is so I can ask her exactly what happened. We're going to find this – this criminal, and Hayley might have some important clues."

He still didn't seem convinced, though after he'd been into the hospital ward and given Hayley a hug and kiss, I saw June beckon him outside, presumably to tell him just what had happened to their daughter.

"Mom's gone ballistic," Hayley greeted me. She was still pale, but brighter eyed now, sitting up in bed with an impressive bandage around her head. "She's feeling guilty I bet because she didn't believe me sooner."

"Will she call the police?" I sat down next to her.

"I hope so! Whoever it was gave me a serious bash-ing, besides stealing my beautiful necklace."

"You didn't see who it was, obviously," I asked

hopefully and she winced a little as she shook her head.

"I didn't stand a chance, Yasmine, he'd set a trap for me. I got to the wood shed and called out for Mom, but it was really quiet, and no one seemed to be around. So I hopped off Sika and went to look inside the shed – it's old, no windows, really dark. I was just peeking in when someone came up behind me and gave me a hard shove, then slammed the door shut and locked it. I yelled and kicked for a bit, and then, oh I don't know how long, it seemed ages later, I heard the lock click and I rushed back outside. I'd tied Sika to a bush but she was gone, so I started running through the woods to find her. I thought I saw something up ahead and was making my way in and out of the trees when I heard a sound behind me. I half turned but he brought his hand down hard. The doctor thinks it was a black-jack, or maybe a small log, and I blacked out."

"You poor thing." I patted her hand gently. "It was definitely a man then, you saw that much?"

"Not really, just a glimpse of someone big and tall. It could have been a woman, I suppose."

My mind was working overtime, trying to work out whom amongst the staff and guests at Black Horse Farm would fit the description. Hayley was looking sleepy, and a nice nurse told me to leave her to get some rest.

"I'll give Sika your love and some extra carrots." I got up to go. "Don't worry about her. We've checked her over really thoroughly."

"Thanks, Yasmine." She yawned widely. "You're very nice, it's no wonder Oliver's so crazy about you."

I blushed immediately and felt a warm glow, but told myself firmly that there was no time for all that. I had to keep a clear mind so Oliver and I could get on with the serious task of solving the mystery of Black Horse Farm.

# Chapter Nine

As soon as I walked back into the big kitchen I could see Oliver was taking it seriously too. With one notebook in front of him he was busy scribbling something into another. He looked up and saw me and gave his fabulous, wobbly-knee-making smile.

"I'm cross referencing," he said rather proudly. "It's been hard pinning anyone down to exact times, but I've got a good general idea."

"You might have to rethink." I flipped his arm casually as I sat beside him. "Hayley was locked in the wood shed before she was attacked, so it's no good looking out for someone who was out of sight for just a minute or two."

"You're kidding!" He stared at me. "Why shut her in there?"

"Beats me." I quickly gave him the whole story as told by Hayley.

"She's sure it was someone big, well tall." Oliver frowned and ran his hand absent-mindedly through the length of my hair.

I almost squirmed with pleasure, but turned my mind back sternly to the problem. "Yes, definitely. I questioned her thoroughly. After all, she's such a little thing, practically everybody here is taller than her."

"Yeah, right." He was still running his fingers through long strands of my hair. "But Jessica, Mandy, Tania, Sue and Emma could hardly be described as tall, even by Hayley's standards. Anyway, they all vouch for each other. They stayed in their groups in view of each other the whole time."

"Who *is* tall and was out of sight at the right time?" It seemed ridiculous to be suspecting any of the other guests, but the height thing was virtually the only clue we had to work with.

"Ah. It seems June's group of five girls stayed together the whole time, just like our group did, but Bill's bunch got split up, I'm not sure how or why. Lee says he took one track, thinking Chas and the rest of them were following, but Bill hadn't made it clear where the next clue led them. They all spent a long time trying to find each other again. Or so they say."

"So they were all riding around on their own," I said slowly. "They could all be suspects if they're tall enough."

"Well, you know their names." Oliver was looking at me closely. "Bill, of course, plus Tania and Jake, who although they got lost, stayed together, and Chas and Lee who, as I've said, got separated."

I knew he was waiting for me to react to Lee's name so I merely said coolly "Let's be methodical. Which of them could be described by Hayley as tall, maybe big?"

"Not Chas, he's a little guy, and Tania's short as well, not as energetic as Hayley and a lot fatter certainly, but definitely not tall."

"So that leaves Bill. He's tall and well-built, but he's Hayley's Dad, so we can rule him out. What about Jake? He's nearly as tall as you, isn't he?" I was disappointed that he'd stopped stroking my hair to start writing again.

"Yes, but he was with Tania all the time, so that puts him in the clear. Then there's Lee…" He stopped scribbling and looked directly at me.

"It couldn't be Lee," I said emphatically. "He's – he's *nice*."

"He *seems* that way, I agree." Oliver leaned back in his chair and put the tips of his fingers together like a judge in a corny old film. "But is he? He was the designated murderer when Hayley got half strangled, remember? And he hangs around her a lot."

"No he doesn't." I just felt it couldn't be Lee.

"Well, a bit maybe, but only because he likes her. He's a really friendly guy."

"Look, you." He grabbed my hand in mock severity. "It's no use saying everyone's far too lovable to have done this, because *someone* bashed Hayley and stole that stupid pendant. We've agreed it must be someone staying at the farm rather than an outsider because of the other attempts."

"Yes, because it seems logical it's been the same person each time an attempt was made to steal the ruby." I frowned and tried counting on my fingers. "So, how many suspects are we talking about? How many people are actually here at Black Horse Farm for a start?"

"There are twelve summer campers including us, plus Hayley herself, of course, her parents, the groom Terry – oh, and the housekeeper Maureen."

"She stayed at the farm while we were treasure hunting, didn't she?"

He shrugged "I suppose so. But we can rule her out anyway. She's a tiny little woman. Even Hayley couldn't describe her as tall."

"Right." I took the pen from his fingers and pulled the notebook towards me. "First we'll write down the members of each group on the treasure hunt, and then we'll make two columns of names based on that. In the first goes anyone tall and big, and in the second any of them who could have sneaked off and attacked Hayley."

"OK." He grinned suddenly. "I love it when you stop being quiet and shy and go all bossy on me."

"Don't be cheeky." I pretended to act like an efficient secretary, holding the notebook for dictation. "And give me the names."

Despite our goofing around we soon had our lists, adding a third column to the "suspects" one. They looked like this:

**Treasure Hunt Groups:**

| Terry | Bill | June |
|-------|------|------|
| Hayley | Jake | Jessica |
| Grant | Tania | Mandy |
| Oliver | Chas | Kelly |
| Yasmine | Lee | Sue |
| | | Emma |

**Suspects:**

| Tall/Big | Opportunity Today | Opportunity Previously |
|----------|-------------------|------------------------|
| Grant | No | Possibly |
| Lee | Yes | Possibly |
| Bill | Yes | Possibly |
| Terry | No | No |
| June | No | Possibly |
| Kelly | No | Possibly |

"If we're adding Kelly to the list I should be on there too." I looked disconsolately at the notebook. "I'm taller than her or June, come to think of it."

"So am I, you dope." He gave me a friendly shove. "But I don't think we need to be in any of the suspect columns, do we?"

"Hmm." I was still staring at the notes. "I wish we hadn't started this. Going with our theory the only two who fit Hayley's description *and* had the chance to attack her are Bill and Lee."

"It can't be Bill. He'd never hurt his own daughter, and if he wanted the ruby pendant he could have gotten it from her easily, just by telling her to hand it over."

"I don't know about that," I argued. "Hayley's as stubborn as a mule sometimes, and she had a real thing about always wearing the ruby. Maybe the way it was stolen was a deliberate ploy to make it seem like it was an outsider rather than her own family."

"Yeah, sure!" He raised his eyebrows. "You can't really believe that – I think you're just determined not to have Lee as the prime suspect."

This was true so I couldn't deny it. I had no reason other than the fact that Lee seemed like such a good guy. I said as much and Oliver got huffy.

"Maybe you'd rather become a detective couple with him if you like him so much. You could put me on the suspects list instead."

"Shut up, you." I pretended to attack him and tried to tickle under his arms. My Mom does it to me sometimes to get me out of a bad mood and it always works. It did the trick with Oliver, too, and we enjoyed quite a squirming marathon, seeing who could tickle the longest. Oliver, being stronger, won and I was so weak with laughing I just couldn't look at the notebook any more. He was grinning as he started reading again, but he suddenly stopped and clapped his hand to his forehead.

"Dope!"

"Who, me?" I struggled to pull myself together.

"No, me. Well, both of us, I guess. Look, we've decided the pendant is valuable, right?"

"It must be, or it wouldn't have been stolen," I said, feeling I was stating the obvious.

"So you think the bank robber bought it with the money he stole and just left it lying here when he was arrested?"

"OK, it seems strange put like that, but maybe he knew the police were on his track and that they'd be looking for a load of cash, and not a cheap-looking necklace."

"Hmm." Oliver wasn't convinced. "Or, of course, it might be nothing to do with the robbery. Maybe it belonged to someone years ago who didn't realize its value."

"Could be," I said. "But I think it's more likely to have been the bank robber's."

"Right, but in either case the pendant is what our thief here wanted, isn't it?"

I thought he'd gone crazy and told him so.

"The point I'm making," he said, trying to sound dignified, "is that the thief has now got what he or she wanted. So there won't be any reason for them to be here any more."

"Brilliant!" I patted his head. "So we just go and find out who's getting ready to leave, do we? Won't they realize that will make them look kind of obvious?"

"Maybe," he nodded. "But they won't want the necklace in their possession. June is bringing the police in, so the thief will want to get rid of it. Let's go and find out who's planning to go off on their own."

It was a logical piece of reasoning, I thought, but when we marched off to find out what everyone was doing, we drew a complete blank. Nearly all the campers were in the kitchen, helping Maureen prepare a load of sandwiches and rolls.

"We're off on a picnic ride," Bill greeted us. "We can't hold classes without June, so we'll have a bit of fun instead."

"Is everyone going?" Oliver asked in surprise.

"Yup. I'll lead the way and you can all ride in pairs

behind me, with Terry bringing up the rear so no one gets lost or separated from the rest."

Oliver raised his eyebrows at me, and Lee, who was reluctantly grating cheese said, "I'd rather stay here and do some more jumping, but Bill says no."

"Terry suggested the outing. It's the only way the two of us can manage all twelve of you. Well, eleven actually, but it'll be good fun, I promise. As soon as June and Hayley are back we'll return to the original schedule."

"Which eleven?" I butted in sharply.

"You and Oliver, Lee, Chas, Jake, Jessica, Mandy, Tania, Kelly, Sue and Emma," he replied patiently.

"So where's Grant?" Oliver was standing close to me and I could feel his muscles tense.

"He's not feeling well." Maureen was working hard preparing sandwich fillings. "He's running a fever, so he's spending the rest of the day in bed. I'll keep an eye on him while you're gone. Come on, Oliver and Yasmine; give a hand with buttering the rolls. Bill and Terry want to get going."

We did as she said, though Oliver muttered, "I don't believe Grant's sick. He could be planning to leave as soon as we're out the way."

"He can't," I whispered back. "Maureen's been told to make sure he stays in bed. Bill just said so. Anyway we *know* it wasn't Grant who stole the pendant., He was with us the whole time, remember."

100

Oliver grunted, but he had to admit I was right. When the food was ready we packed it into saddle-bags, tacked up the horses, and set off. Now that everyone knew Hayley was OK they were all cheerful. Bill hadn't told them about her being hit, so no one seemed worried. The only ones not laughing and chatting away were Bill, who was obviously upset about Hayley, Oliver and I, deep in 'detecting' thought, Lee, who still wanted to stay and practice jumping – oh, and Terry, of course because he was always morose. We'd gone quite a distance across the downs when behind us the groom suddenly got off the bay cob and ran his hand down the off fore.

"He seems a bit lame," he explained so we all halted and Bill rode back from the front of the line.

"Trot him out," he ordered, and Terry ran beside the cob so we could see how he was moving.

The poor horse was indeed very lame on that leg, and I saw Bill's brow pucker even further. "We'll have to go back."

"No, that'll spoil everyone's fun." The big, balding groom seemed to be trying hard to please for once. "I'll walk him back on my own. You all carry on and enjoy yourselves."

"I'll come with you," Lee said eagerly but Bill clapped him on the shoulder and said, "Oh no, I'm not having you doing jumping practice on your own. You

come up in front with me and we'll find a few logs and stuff to jump on the way."

Oliver turned to me, his eyes gleaming. "See? He's been trying to get out of coming with us from the start."

"Terry?" I didn't understand. "But we know it can't be Terry. We've been through all this."

"You know I don't mean him. You've got to accept it, Yasmine. The thief can only be one person – the one person we worked out earlier – tall enough and with the opportunity to ride off alone and attack Hayley – it's Lee, Yasmine, it's got to be Lee!"

# Chapter Ten

I wouldn't look at him. Instead I stared straight ahead to where Lee and Chas rode side-by-side, laughing and talking with Kelly and Emma.

"Say something!" Oliver sounded really annoyed. "And not your usual, 'Oh, Lee's too nice, it can't be him.'"

"Well he is, and it can't," I said stubbornly.

"But apart from Bill he's the only one it could be!" Oliver was nearly shouting.

"We must have worked it out all wrong." I wasn't going to be bullied. "Maybe we should look at it from another angle."

"What angle? Unless it was some kind of conspiracy between the others, all giving each other an alibi, only your precious Lee was alone at the right time, apart from Bill, that is, and we've ruled him out."

"That could be it!" I stamped firmly on the lovely

glowing realization that Oliver was a bit jealous of Lee, and concentrated hard. "I can't believe a whole group would be involved in Hayley's attack but if, say Jake and Tania were working together – "

"What d'you mean – that Tania locked Hayley in the shed, then let her out so Jake could bash her?" He was being sarcastic, of course, but I nodded.

"There must be something that would explain the whole shed thing. Tania might have shut Hayley in there because she, Tania I mean, is too little to have socked her."

"But if they were together why didn't Jake do the hitting there and then?" Oliver was frowning, giving my idea serious thought at last.

"I don't know," I admitted. "It doesn't make sense. But then the fact that Hayley was locked in the shed at all doesn't make sense, does it?"

"No, all it does is mess up the timing when we try to work out which of the suspects did it."

"In which case maybe that was the point behind it, to confuse the issue so that whoever did the bashing appeared to have an alibi when he actually didn't because Hayley was attacked later than we first thought." It sounded confused even as I was saying it and Oliver grinned.

"Clear as mud, Yasmine! You'll be telling me next the body we saw lying on the ground wasn't Hayley at all – it was some other girl who just happened to be a slim blonde dressed in a pink jumper and – "

"Stop!" I said urgently. "Something went click in my brain when you said that."

Oliver obligingly brought Lincoln to a halt and watched my face as I tried to work it out. The other riders, unaware we were no longer behind them, began to disappear out of sight, still laughing and talking together.

"We ought to catch up – " Oliver began, but I held up my hand and said, "Give me a minute. I'm sure I can do it."

It was very quiet now that the others had gone, with only birdsong and the occasional sound of our ponies blowing through their noses as they stood waiting patiently in the dappled shade.

"That's it!" I got Flint to do a perfect turn on the forehand. "Come on!"

"Where – what –?" Oliver spun Lincoln and began cantering after me. "Yasmine, where are we going?"

"Back to the farm," I called over my shoulder. "And quick!"

"Shouldn't we let Bill know?" He was beside me now, his bay horse keeping perfect time with Flint.

"There's no time." I felt my teeth set grimly. "We've got to stop them getting away."

"Who?" Oliver was deeply puzzled.

I couldn't resist showing off my detective skills. "It was you talking about some other girl in a pink sweater. Tell me what we saw when we found Hayley."

He checked Lincoln's speed and looked over at me as if I'd gone mad. "You know what we saw. Hayley lying on the ground unconscious."

"Describe her," I said, to his obvious irritation.

"She was face down, her arms in that pink sweater thing were flung out, her hat was off and her hair was all tumbled around her shoulders."

"Face down," I repeated. "So how did we know it was Hayley?"

"Don't be crazy. Who else could it be? Anyway, Terry rushed straight to her and turned her face towards him."

"Exactly," I said smugly. "And that's who we're chasing now. Look ahead – who do you see?"

Shaking his head in disbelief he did as I asked. "No one."

"And if the horse Terry was riding really was lame, we'd see the pair of them plodding their way home."

"That's true." Oliver looked at me with growing respect. "I'm being thick, I guess, so you'll have to tell me exactly how it all happened."

"Right." I was slightly out of breath but managed to speak clearly. "You, me, Grant, Terry and Hayley are together when Terry's phone rings. He tells Hayley it's her Mom wanting to meet up with her. Because we think Grant is the danger we let Hayley ride off and the four of us stay together and hunt for the next clue. In the meantime Hayley reaches the shed and instead of seeing her Mom she is shoved inside and locked in. The person who did that then runs through the woods and lies down in an agreed spot. She's wearing an identical sweater and pants and –" I paused for effect, "– A blonde wig."

"A blonde – " Oliver nearly fell off. "So when we arrive on the scene we're met with a picture that tells us it's Hayley lying there!"

"Terry sends us all off, then the person in the wig leaps up, runs back to the shed, sets Sika cantering off and releases Hayley. That means Terry can wait 'til the girl reaches the right place, then he hits her from behind and takes the pendant from around her neck."

"And when you got back with June there was Hayley, conscious now, with Terry still pretending to be looking after her."

"It gave Terry the perfect alibi. With our evidence no one could suspect him, and of course no one realized that he had this accomplice."

The farm was now in view but there was still no sight of the groom.

"So who was she?" Oliver was agog. "Not Tania,

surely? She's the right height but too plump, and anyway Jake was with her the whole time. The other girls were all together, too, so who – " He broke off, a frown creasing his forehead.

"Go on," I said encouragingly. "Who's small and slight enough to pass as a face-down Hayley?"

He groaned and said, "I'm trying to imagine each girl in a blonde wig. It's no use, I give up!"

"Maureen," I said simply. "It's got to be Maureen."

Oliver stared at me for a moment. "And Terry's galloped back to meet her so they can take the pendant and run?"

"That's how I see it," I agreed. "Terry must have jammed a stone in his horse's hoof to make it look lame. I suppose he knew he and Maureen couldn't just take off after Hayley's attack. We'd have realized they were guilty right away and stopped them."

"Incredible! You're brilliant to have worked it all out, Yasmine, but what if we're too late? They're probably gone."

We'd slowed the pace now and were riding quietly through the belt of trees at the side of the farmhouse. To our right was a lawn, which stretched through to the front garden, separated from the outside lane by a solid growth of tall hedgerow. We began peering through the woods, hoping to catch a glimpse of Terry's truck, which would mean we weren't too late.

To our utter amazement what we *did* see was the groom himself, stripped to the waist as he dug ferociously at a spot two thirds of the way along the lawn. Next to him, working more slowly and with a deeply resentful expression on his face, was Grant. I nearly let out a squeak of surprise and Oliver put his finger against my mouth.

"Ssh. We've got to get the police. I'll sneak into the house and phone."

"I'll come with you." I hooked Flint's reins over the same branch as Lincoln's and followed Oliver, nervously creeping through the cover of trees. We were OK 'til we reached the last one; ahead was an open stretch about twenty yards long leading to the front door of the house.

"You stay here," Oliver hissed. "Keep out of sight and I'll make a run for it."

Before I could argue he'd taken off, sprinting swiftly for the house. I thought he was going to make it, then to my horror Terry looked up and spotted him. Throwing down his spade he gave a great roar and started running heavily across the lawn towards him. He was surprisingly fast and my heart plummeted at the thought he might catch Oliver and beat him up – or worse. Rashly I sprang forward and began running in the opposite direction, back towards the horses and away from the farmhouse, out in the open and in clear view of the angry groom. He saw me immediately and, as I hoped, veered towards me.

"Maureen will take care of the boy," he yelled to Grant. "Help me catch this one before she can raise the alarm."

I hadn't bargained on Grant. I was running towards him, not directly as he was still standing beside the hole they'd been digging on the far side of the lawn, but all he had to do was sprint across the grass and he'd cut me off from getting back to the horses. I saw him throw down his spade and desperately tried to increase my speed, but after one uncertain step, Grant stayed where he was, ignoring the curses from Terry, who continued to chase after me. I was nearly at the place we'd tied the horses – I just had to weave between the trees and there they were, waiting patiently. Terry was obviously fitter than he looked and was rapidly gaining on me, so I knew I had to act fast. Making a flying leap on to Flint's back was super easy for me. I'd done it a thousand times in our pony club games, but there was also the problem of Lincoln. I realized if I left the bay horse Terry would climb aboard and come galloping after me. Lincoln's incredibly fast and I knew he'd catch me, but there was no way I could simply release him and let him go belting off on his own in case he got hurt. The only possible solution was to take *both* horses with me.

I called Flint's name so he wouldn't be scared, and as he turned his beautiful black head to look at me I vaulted into his saddle, leaning forward and unhooking both his and Lincoln's reins from the branch. Flat out gallop wasn't possible through the closely packed trees, and I could hear Terry's curses and the heavy sound of his running feet as he kept on coming after us. But then we were out in the open and I urged Flint on, cantering powerfully across the broad sweep of lawn with Lincoln pounding alongside. The two horses' heads were almost level. I had a set of reins in each hand and was praying the big bay wouldn't veer away or, worse still, come to a sudden stop. Terry's yells were getting fainter and I knew we were getting away from him but then I realized to my horror that to reach the comparative safety of the driveway we'd have to gallop past Grant who was still standing at the side of the hole he and Terry had been digging. I knew he could have stopped me earlier, but I didn't dare risk taking the horses close to him. The only way out was to change direction and head instead for the formidable looking hedge, which separated the garden from the lane outside. It was higher than anything Flint and I had attempted to jump so far, and for an instant my knees turned to water at the thought of trying to clear it with *two* horses.

I gritted my teeth, then made a conscious effort to

relax and sit quietly as we pounded nearer and nearer the solid green height. The merest touch on my wonderful horse's flanks and we were soaring up and up, Lincoln's handsome bay head still in line with Flint's as we literally flew over, to land, almost perfectly, on the thick covering of grass in the lane outside. Flint pecked slightly but recovered immediately, and although I felt as though my left arm was about to come out of its socket I still held on to Lincoln's reins as we slowed the pace of our frantic canter. It was Flint, bless him, who warned me we weren't out of danger, neighing loudly as we eased our way along the grass verge of the lane. I glanced hurriedly round and saw to my terror that Terry's beat-up old pickup truck was roaring out of Black Horse Farm's drive, tires squealing as he turned sharply towards us.

Both horses were magnificent, galloping their hearts out as I tried to get away. The lane is a long one and there were no other houses on it, I knew, and I also knew I couldn't hope to outrun the fast approaching truck. I kept the horses galloping anyway, crouching low over Flint's neck and doing my best to help him keep up with Lincoln's longer stride. The siren, when it came, was like the clarion call of an angel. I heard it, faint at first, becoming gloriously louder as the police car came speeding towards us. Terry, who was by now so close I could see the ugly scowl on the

face behind the pickup's wheel, heard it too. For a horrible moment I thought he was going to ignore it and actually run the three of us down. A picture flashed into my mind, a dreadful image of brave and beautiful horses crushed and mangled beneath the truck's wheels.

Then, with a great clashing of gears and the smell of burning rubber, Terry threw the truck into a spin, bouncing across the opposite verge to face the other way. He nearly made it, and presumably would have driven straight for the approaching police car in an effort to bulldoze it off the road. Instead the engine screamed and then died, shuddering drunkenly to a halt as it stalled. Terry leapt out and began running across the fields, followed swiftly by two policemen from the car.

At last I could stop, and I slowed Flint and Lincoln gratefully, feeling as if every nerve in my body had been stretched and pummeled. I slid off my horse's back and the three of us stood there on the lush covering of grass, leaning thankfully into each other as we tried to recover from the terrible chase. Breathlessly I watched the tallest of the policemen gradually gain on Terry until at last he was captured. I could see the glint of handcuffs as the police began to lead him back to their patrol car, and I heaved a sigh of relief and started walking the horses slowly back towards

Black Horse Farm. We'd gone a good few yards when Flint gave his warning neigh and I saw, to my unspeakable horror, that Grant, holding a spade as if it was a weapon, had emerged from the trees and was coming straight for me!

## Chapter Eleven

I gulped frantically and tried to decide whether I had time to leap back aboard Flint and gallop away. The trouble was I was pretty sure I didn't have a leap left in me; I'd gone all limp and wobbly once I thought the danger had passed. I must have showed something of this in my face because Grant loosened his grip on the shovel's handle and let it drop harmlessly to the ground.

"What – what are you doing?" I stammered, still feeling horribly nervous.

"I came to make sure he didn't hurt you."

"Oh." I blinked in surprise. "The spade was meant to defend me?"

He nodded, dropping his eyes.

"Well, thanks." It sounded like a dumb thing to say, so I added hurriedly, "Though I don't suppose I should be thanking you, after seeing you help Terry.

What were you digging for, and how come you were involved anyway? He's a crook; you must know that. He and Maureen were the ones who bashed Hayley and stole the pendant."

"I know," he said quietly. "And I know they're both criminals. I should – they're my parents."

To say I was dumbstruck is putting it mildly. I goggled at him like a googly-eyed goldfish. "Your m-m-mother and father?"

He nodded again, his dark face closed and shuttered. "I'll walk with you and give myself up to the police."

I stared at him. "I worked out how Terry and Maureen tricked us, but what did you have to do with the attack?"

"Nothing." His eyes were still hooded. "Look, Yasmine, I'll tell you the story from the beginning. You deserve at least that, and – and maybe you'll pass it on to Hayley so she'll know I'm sorry."

"Sorry!" The enormity of the fact that he was involved had begun to sink in, but he held up a hand and said, "This is how it happened. My Dad, Terry to you, has been in and out of prison loads of times, and during the last stretch he shared a cell for a while with the guy who used to own Black Horse Farm."

"The bank robber," I put in.

"Yes. He was sick, and died soon after, but one night before they took him off to the hospital, he was delirious and kept talking about a map he'd made. Dad knew the guy was inside for stealing this huge stash of money that had never been found, so he listened pretty carefully. When he was released, Dad, I mean, he couldn't wait to rush over to this Black Horse Farm and start searching for the map."

"But the farm had been sold. The Prestons had bought it and were turning it into a pony summer camp," I said, with him so far.

"Yeah. The only way to get access was to join the place, me as a riding guest, knocking three years off my age – "

"You're eighteen," I said cleverly, and he nodded again.

"Mom applied for the job as housekeeper, forged herself some brilliant references, moved in and started 'spring cleaning' the house from top to bottom as an excuse for map hunting. I was told to become very pally with Hayley so I could get access to the Prestons' private rooms, and Dad got the job as groom, which meant he could spend his time searching the stables and barns."

"How did he manage to get the job of groom?" I asked curiously "He was useless at it."

"Mom destroyed all the other applications," Grant said simply. "And they forged glowing references again."

"Right, so there you all were, tearing the place apart in your search for the map. Where do Hayley and the pendant come into the story?"

"We'd nearly given up, couldn't find a thing, then Hayley announced she'd found the pendant on the day they moved in, and we realized what that meant. At first I was as keen as my parents. It didn't seem like any big deal to waltz off with a load of money we hadn't actually stolen, so I tried hard to get the necklace off Hayley."

"It was you who spooked Sika into bolting that day," I realized. "Was that one of your plans to get Hayley on her own?"

"Yeah." He hung his head. "I told my parents that once I got Hayley alone I could easily sneak the pendant away from her, but I didn't get the chance. Mom tried stealing her clothes while we were in the sea, but that was no good because Hayley was wearing the necklace. It was my fault, really. She'd spotted me trying to steal it from her room and her guard was up."

"And the other night?" I looked at him fiercely. "Was that you who nearly strangled Hayley?"

He rubbed a hand across his eyes. "It was horrible. My Mom and Dad told me I had to use the Murder game as an opportunity to sneak up behind her and wrench the thing off her neck. I honestly didn't know it was on a piece of leather. I thought I'd give it one quick tug and it would break. Instead the leather bit into her neck, and it wasn't until she started making those choking noises I realized what was happening. I let go right away and I told my parents I was through, and that I wouldn't help them get the pendant if it meant hurting anybody."

"So you didn't know about the trap they set up for Hayley in the wood shed?"

He shook his head. "No, I swear I didn't. When we rode into the woods and saw that little body lying there I honestly thought Hayley had fallen off Sika and hurt her head. Dad had been in full sight of you, Oliver, and me so he couldn't be responsible. It was only when I heard everyone say she'd been locked in the shed and *then* attacked and the pendant stolen, that I realized my dear Mom and Dad had been behind it. Honestly, Yasmine I wanted to tell the police everything, even then, but they wouldn't let me. They said that in a few hours we'd have the money and be able to live like kings from now on."

"Have the money?" I was puzzled. "We thought the pendant *was* the money. What were you digging for in the garden?"

He looked at me and a small smile lightened his dark face. "You were really clever to work out how they rigged up the attack on Hayley. I'd have thought you'd discover the pendant's secret too."

"Well, I didn't," I said irritably. "So tell me."

"You can see for yourself." To my amazement he reached in a pocket and drew out the sea green necklace, with its red stone sparkling brightly.

We were now plodding up the drive of Black Horse Farm and ahead I could see the police car with Terry and Maureen sitting in the back seat looking furious while the driver of another car stood listening to the tall policeman who'd caught Terry. To my great relief Oliver was there too, talking anxiously to someone I thought was probably the Chief of Police. In fact he was a detective, but I was close. They all turned to look as we appeared around the curve in the drive, and Oliver started running towards me.

"Yasmine! Are you OK? I can't believe you made that incredible jump – and with both horses!"

"I had a pretty good teacher." I smiled at him and the grin I got back made my poor old wobbly knees turn to jelly again.

"Here." Grant spoke quietly to me. "You'll have to give it in as evidence, but take the pendant. There's a map on the kitchen table – go and solve the final mystery."

I closed my hand over the pendant and handed Lincoln's reins to Oliver, who bent forward and kissed me. On the cheek, admittedly, but it was near enough to my mouth to be interesting.

"Come on." I hurried past the waiting policemen who were moving forward to deal with Grant. "There's something I have to do."

We hitched our reins over a post and rushed into the house. Oliver gave me a hug and told me he'd been terrified thinking what Terry would do if he caught me.

"No fear of that," I said, clamping down the tremor I felt when I remembered the big man coming after me. "How did you get the police here so quickly? And what did you do with Maureen?"

"When I dialed 911 they said a car was already on its way because of what Hayley had told them. They only had to radio it and get it to speed up a bit."

"I just loved the sound of that siren," I admitted. "And Maureen?"

"Oh, I gave her some of her own back," he said, grinning. "She came at me and I bundled her neatly into a cupboard and locked the door. As soon as I'd phoned I went running down the drive to try and rescue you, but then I heard the siren too. Pretty soon the second police car picked me up and told me you were OK."

"I'm fine," I reaffirmed, feeling a lovely squiggle of pleasure that he'd been prepared to tackle the crooks for me. "And Oliver, although Grant *was* involved he refused to be part of any violence so I hope he gets treated leniently."

I gave him a quick resume of everything Grant had told me and by now we'd reached the kitchen. Sure enough, there on the table was a big map of the area.

"Look." I traced my finger along the line. "Here's the lane outside, and this is the boundary of Black Horse Farm."

"So it is." Oliver leaned in very close as he studied the map.

It was nice, but I had other things on my mind.

"Got it," I said suddenly. "This is the front garden – see this curving line here? And that's about where Flint, Lincoln and I jumped the hedge, just past where Terry and Grant were digging."

"That jump was amazing," Oliver said, frowning. "But I don't get *why* they were digging. I thought once they got the pendant they'd be off."

"No, it was the *map* they'd been looking for – a map showing exactly where the bank robber had hidden the money. He thought he'd be coming back in a few years to collect it."

"I don't understand – " Oliver began, then drew in his breath as I produced the pendant.

Carefully I put it in place, the wavy contours of the blue green glass fitting precisely into the shape of the farm's front garden.

"And there, exactly where the little red stone is," I said, and Oliver let out his breath in a great gust.

"The red stone marks the place they were digging! It's not a ruby – *the pendant itself* is the map!"

Oliver took me in his arms and held me close, and I remember thinking happily that I had so much to look forward to, now that we'd at last solved the mystery at Black Horse Farm.